W9-CCE-512

The Assassin's Heart

The
Assassin's Heart

~~~

J.A. Kazimer

Seattle, WA

MAIN LIBRARY
Champaign Public Library
200 West Green Street
Champaign, Illinois 61820-5193

Chapter 1

~~

Arrowland Theme Park, Sonoran Desert, AZ
18May, 1600 hours

A MAN APPEARED BETWEEN the crosshairs of the sniper scope, but Six held her position. Waiting for the signal. Always waiting. The harsh heat of the sun beat down upon her. Sweat drenched her back, soaking her running shorts. Still, she waited, unmoving, even though the Barrett M82 rifle in her arms weighed over thirty pounds. The stench of rancid oil, fear, and puke wafted through the air, breaching her sniper's nest. Her stomach roiled, but her finger remained poised on the trigger.

Six was used to the heavy load, the waiting, and even the unbearable heat. Rigorous training kept her thin and capable of enduring a lot more than this. Sometimes introspection crept in. Given her cold-blooded efficiency, that happened rarely. She would wonder what the hell she was doing in the middle of a desert, sweating her butt off for a few thousand dollars a month. There had to be a better way to make a living, one that didn't involve bullets, brains, and bloodshed.

The radio in her ear crackled to life. "Not our target," Benjamin Miller, her partner, drawled. "What'd you say we call it a day? Grab a snow-cone and ride the Cyclone?"

As hot as she was, she refused to give up now. The target would fall. Their mission would be accomplished. Six and Ben would collect their money and move on to another job in another hellhole. That was life. Her life. The one chosen for her many years ago.

When she didn't answer, Ben tried again. "C'mon. The guy ain't showing. I'm hot, tired, and hungry. We can start fresh in the morning."

Fresh, yeah right. She would never be fresh again, not after four days of sweating her ass off in one hundred degree desert heat waiting to kill a man while Ben sat inside an air-conditioned Jeep hundreds of yards away from any danger, let alone the bone-shearing heat. He probably smelled as fresh as a daisy, while she—she sniffed her armpit—stunk like wet badger fur and gym socks. The costume's fur was actually synthetic, but it smelled as rank as the real thing. What did it matter to Ben if she'd spent the last eight hours developing heat rash on every part of her body?

She imagined him sitting there, rapping out a silent tune on the steering wheel with one hand and raking the other through his curly dark hair, his jeans and T-shirt clinging to his lean, muscular body. With his Scots-Irish dark hair and green eyes, he was always ready for his close-up in a gangster flick, whereas she .... Well, she looked okay when she wasn't sweating like a wart hog in a badger costume. Although pink wasn't her most flattering hair color.

From her sniper's roost, she poked the furry middle finger of her left hand into the air to show Ben just what she thought of his idea. The finger on her right hand stayed steady on the trigger.

His laughter floated through the radio. "Watch it or you'll be spending your weekend in sensitivity training." He waited a beat. "Again."

"Ever heard of radio silence?" she asked. "Pros use it to keep the element of surprise on their side." She fought a grin. "Not that you'd know anything about that."

"Funny, but I was about to say the same about you," he said, his tone turning serious. "According to the GPS tracker, our target just popped his head up from the tunnel four seconds ago. You wanna take the shot so we can go home? I've got money on the Coyotes' game tonight."

Damn it. She swung her attention back to the smooth lines of the crosshairs on her scope. Her heartbeat accelerated, but outwardly she showed no signs of stress. "Are you sure it's him?" She blinked, unable to tell if the man was indeed their target.

"It's him," he assured her. "Now shoot the bastard so we can go home."

"You got it," she said, her finger adjusting the pressure on the trigger.

Breathe in. Slow. Steady.

Just like they taught her.

Hold.

Fire.

The bullet ripped through the air, silenced by distance and the delighted screams of children. Colors whirled together, spinning faster and faster as the round spiraled toward its victim with deadly accuracy.

Ricky the Rabbit never knew what hit him. One minute his enlarged, fluffy head popped out of an underground passage, and the next, his pink bunny fur ran red with blood.

From fifty-feet above, Six, dressed in sixty pounds of a Buffy the Badger costume, lowered her sniper rifle, yanked off her badger head and gulped in a burst of hot desert air. She shook her head, eyes scanning the amusement park. "Friendliest place on Earth, my ass."

Chapter 2

~

B EN GRINNED AS THE terrorist rabbit fell. Say what you will about Six, she got the job done. No question. The bunny was dead. Their mission was complete. The threat to America and Arizona's Arrowland Theme Park was no more.

Of course, even with the rabbit dead, his job was far from done. The target was down, sure, but now it was time for cleanup. The American public must never find out how close they'd come to mass destruction and, with Ben on the job, they never would. His meticulous attention to every detail and his unwavering belief in good versus evil made him the perfect assassin, albeit a lousy husband. Or, so his ex-wife had declared shortly after their Vegas wedding.

Ben slammed the Jeep into gear, racing between the Monster Coaster and Flash Mountain down the vacant Frontier Trail where the blood-soaked bunny lay hidden behind an electrical box.

The Jeep screeched to a stop, narrowly missing the Tiny, Tiny, Teacup ride. This part of the park was deserted, thanks to lame rides like The Paddle Wheel Boat (top speed three miles per hour) and the Space Needle, the one attraction where you could actually feel the seconds tick off your life.

The park patrons never knew how important Frontier Trail was to every aspect of their fun family adventure. Twisted miles of tunnels, electronics, and security lay beneath the trail, strategically placed to keep its patrons safe, stuffed, and happy. The trail was like the brain of Arrowland Theme Park, quietly computing all day long while the body enjoyed corn dogs and candy apples.

The rabbit used this information.

In fact, Ricky the Rabbit, or John Pillars(as he was known in his CIA file) knew a lot about Arrowland. As Ricky the Rabbit, he could and did move unnoticed throughout the miles of underground tunnels owned by the park, hiding an arsenal of weapons for sale to the highest bidder. No one was ever the wiser. Until last month, when Ricky the Rabbit had joined the CIA's Ten Most Wanted.

After Arrowland Theme Park learned of John's less than noble activities, the CEO immediately contacted OPS, a corporation of security experts run by the CIA, to evaluate the risk to apple pie and the American way.

Once the threat level was assessed, OPS did what any corporation did in a time of crisis; it outsourced the job to two of their finest assassins. That was how Ben found himself tugging the dead body of the popular rabbit into the plush leather of his Jeep.

Damn bunny weighed a ton.

Ben yanked the bunny by his unlucky foot, the muscles in his well-developed arms and legs bulging under the weight. The sun beat down on his broad back, staining his Sex Pistols T-shirt with perspiration. Sweat plastered the dark hair to his head in tiny ringlets. On anyone else the baby fine ringlets would've looked childish, but not on him. Benjamin Miller was pure testosterone.

The jaded intelligence in his green eyes covered by a pair of dark glasses suggested a lifetime, crammed into the span of thirty-two years. This was a soldier who made his living from the death of others. A task the normally laid-back assassin failed to take lightly.

He pulled at the bunny, moving the body a few more inches toward the Jeep. Blood soaked into the blacktop, its coppery stench disturbing a swarm of flies nesting nearby. They buzzed around, ignoring Ben and his threats of total fly annihilation. "Where the hell is Six when I need her?" he asked, glancing around for any sign of his slacker of a partner.

He instantly spotted her, her legs dangling fifty feet in the air as she rappelled from the Badger Bonanza Stage, a long black case tucked under her arm.

Unfortunately, he wasn't the only one to take notice. A group of teenage boys also stared, with something akin to reverence, at the vision slowly slithering down the thick rope.

And who could blame them? Dressed in a sweat-soaked black sports bra and a pair of equally wet running shorts, she looked like the chick from *Tomb Raider* come to life. Her short pink hair and toned body only added to the videogame inspired fantasy.

He shook his head. Six was just too beautiful for her own good. It made men, bad men like him, want to take advantage. Of course messing with her could be costly. The girl could take out a man at 1,000 yards, not to mention the pleasure she took in doing just that. She was hardcore assassin all the way. Business always came first. Kill the target and get out. Hell, after three years, Ben barely thought of her as a woman. Or so he told himself every time he caught her scent—something flowery with a hint of sex. A scent that heated his blood and tightened his body.

Six planted her feet on the ground and started to jog toward the Jeep. Glancing from the downed bunny to his partner, he blew out a harsh breath. "I need a vacation."

"Yeah, right," she said through the radio. "You live for the job."

He frowned. It didn't used to be like that. He'd had a life, once upon a time. Friends. A wife. A dog. Damn, he missed that dog. Now he spent months at a time traveling to far-off places, places better left untraveled, for a price.

A hefty price.

Some nights, in the pitch black darkness, he wondered if it was all worth it, if he brought any order to the chaos in the world, if killing one bad man really mattered.

With morning came clarity as the news reports of another terrorist attack, school shooting, or innocent life lost flickered across the screen. Whatever he'd done or might do in the future, Ben saved lives.

You had to break a few eggs to make an omelet … or keep the world safe. Right?

⊕

SIX WHOLEHEARTEDLY AGREED WITH Ben's egg-breaking worldview, at least she did for the next seven minutes.

"Grab his arms," Ben said when she arrived at the scene of the assassination. She did as he asked, grunting a little under the bunny's weight. Ben raised an eyebrow.

She blushed, wishing she'd bit her tongue off rather than show any sign of weakness. Being a woman in the male-dominated field of assassination was hard enough without Ben's constant scrutiny and machismo. A male assassin could have an off-day, maybe miss a mark by a quarter inch, but not her. She had to be on target all the time. Forget feeling bloated or bitchy. Forget emotions, PMS, or chocolate cravings. To Ben, she wasn't a woman, but a tool. Nothing more than the number six, a nickname she'd earned the day she partnered with Ben. Gone was her former self, Hannah Winslow—woman, treasured daughter, loyal friend—replaced by a single numeral without a past or the promise of a normal life beyond the barrel of a gun. And now she thought of herself as 'Six' as well.

She sighed at the thought. Sometimes she dreamed of fancy lace dresses and high-heeled fuck-me boots, of going on a real date with a 'real' man whose intentions went beyond stabbing the spy at the next table before the dessert course. But it wasn't to be. This was her life, a life spent making the world a better place, and she loved it, most days.

Together, Ben and Six maneuvered the bloody rabbit into the plastic-wrapped backseat of the Jeep. Once the bunny was safely buckled up, Ben jumped into the driver's seat. "Hop in."

She rolled her eyes at the pun.

But he wasn't finished. With a grin he motioned to the backseat and the bloody guy in a bunny suit. "He won't bite."

She stifled a sigh. "I thought our orders were for you to stay here and do recon and for me to drive the bunny out of the park?" Her sapphire-colored eyes traveled from the dead man back to Ben, a man as deadly as the bunny was dead.

"Change of plans. Parker's orders. He wants us both on the road ASAP. Must have another job for us." He was referring to their boss. Ben grinned, his teeth looking especially sharp in the barren landscape.

"But…" she began, a chill teasing her sweat-soaked skin. Why the sudden change of plans? Was Ben keeping something from her? It wouldn't be the first time. *Damn him.*

"We need to go. Now," Ben said, his tone leaving little room for questions.

Six wasn't afraid of much. Spiders didn't scare her, neither did snakes or the occasional bad date. Benjamin Miller was a different story. She'd witnessed his skills first hand. His speed and strength. His willingness to kill to complete a mission. In a perfect world there would be no need for men like Miller. But this world was far from perfect.

"What about—" she began.

"I took care of it. Now get in the Jeep," he ordered in a timbre she'd never quite heard before, fraught with unmistakable tension.

"Did something happen?"

He sighed loud enough to wake the dead bunny. "What's with the twenty questions? We need to move out. That's all."

"Fine." Inspecting his face for signs of something amiss, she tossed her sniper rifle into the backseat and climbed in after it.

He smiled grimly, jamming the Jeep into gear. "We'll head toward the west exit. It's been under construction for a week. Should be an easy out."

Six didn't doubt it. Ben knew exactly what to do and he did it without hesitation. Every eventuality had been planned for, every escape route checked twice.

THE JEEP CAREENED OVER a bump, sending the bloody bunny bouncing toward her. She reached out to steady him and instead she dislodged his big, brain-splattered stuffed head. It flopped off the seat and rolled onto the floor, spreading a red smear across the Jeep's interior.

She paid little heed to the mess of congealing blood. Instead she focused on the face underneath the rabbit head. "Ben?"

"What?"

"We've got a problem." The calmness of her voice amazed her. She sounded so normal, as if discussing the hot weather, when, in fact, her heart had lodged in her throat and time had slowed to a crawl.

"What's up?" he asked, his eyes catching hers in the rearview mirror. For a few seconds, silent communication seemed to pass between the two of them. The tension in the Jeep increased.

She cleared her throat. "This isn't our target. This isn't John Pillars." Even with half of his face missing she recognized the man in the bunny suit. *Oh God, no. Not Davis.*

Bile rose in her throat, choking the normally untouchable assassin as she stared into the dead eyes of OPS agent Davis Karter, a man she had kissed goodbye only three nights earlier.

The Jeep slowed. Ben half-turned in the driver's seat. His eyes roamed over Davis' face, inspecting every inch. He resumed driving.

"Say something," she said, her voice cracking.

"He's the least of our problems," Ben said, nodding to the blood-soaked bunny's left paw and the timer with a two-minute countdown on it.

Chapter 3

～

BEN SLOWED THE JEEP and over his shoulder said, "Switch." Offering no argument, Six maneuvered her lithe body over the backseat and into the passenger seat. He hefted his frame from the driver's seat, kicking his long legs over the smooth leather, narrowly missing the side of her head.

Like a Ziploc baggie, the two assassins acted as one, keeping the danger inside the Jeep contained. She grabbed the wheel, slipped under him and into the driver's seat. The Jeep barely slowed. Ben ended up in the backseat next to the bloodied and wired bunny.

With great care, he ripped open the bunny costume, exposing a tangle of wires and C-4 beneath. He let out a soft whistle.

"That bad, huh?" she asked, glancing in the rearview mirror. She noted the beads of sweat on Ben's forehead and swallowed hard before returning her attention to the road. The Jeep's tires kicked up dust and dirt but, with the exception of a few cacti standing vigil alongside, the road was empty. A good thing too since the amount of C-4 strapped to the bunny could leave a good-size crater if detonated. *When detonated*, she thought.

They needed to get farther from civilization, farther from

innocent victims riding a tilt-a-whirl only a few miles away, farther into the deserted desert.

She pushed harder on the gas pedal, swerving to avoid a pothole in the center of the road. Even the slightest jolt could blow the bunny, the Jeep, and the two assassins sky high.

They didn't have much time. That much was apparent. Ben was skilled, very skilled, but disarming a bomb with a pocketknife while traveling at seventy miles per hour went beyond the typical 'day in the life.'

"Damn," he whispered, causing Six to wince.

"What do you need?"

He shot her a quick grin in the rearview mirror. "A beer would be nice. Hell, let's go for a whole six-pack."

"You disconnect that bomb and I'll buy you a case."

"Deal. Six …." His tone was serious, far more than she was used to. She struggled to maintain her grip on the wheel, wanting more than anything to turn to her partner and tell him everything would be all right. That, no matter what, they would survive. They had to. They were the good guys.

Or were they?

Davis.

Six shook her head, trying not to think about the dead agent in the backseat. Or the fact she'd been the one to shoot him less than thirty minutes earlier. Instead, she stayed quiet, her hands at ten and two on the steering wheel.

"Do me a favor," Ben said.

"Anything," she said without hesitation.

"Jump."

"What?"

He repeated his statement. "I said, jump. Slow the Jeep, and on my command jump out of the damn vehicle. I can probably buy enough time to get clear of the blast, but you have to move fast."

"But—"

"That's an order." His voice softened. "Listen Six, this ain't gonna end well. The bunny's loaded with C-4 and we're running out of time."

Through the whirl of the Jeep's air conditioner she heard the telltale click of seconds ticking by on the timer. She swung to face the clock. Thirty seconds.

Her eyes cut to Ben's.

"Slow it down," he ordered. "Now."

With a deep breath she turned to face the road again, her foot slipping from the gas pedal to the brake. The Jeep lurched in response but failed to slow. Instead the engine revved, sending the speedometer shooting to ninety miles per hour. She slammed her foot harder on the brake. The pedal hit the floorboard with little result.

"Shit," he said, his voice surprisingly calm. "Okay, plan B."

"It better be a hell of a lot better than plan A," she said, yanking the key from the ignition as she pulled the emergency brake in hopes of slowing the runaway vehicle. The Jeep's speed dropped to seventy-five, and then quickly accelerated again.

"Not really," he said. "Same plan with one exception."

"What's that?"

"Tuck and roll, sweetheart. On three," he said, his voice sounding distant over the blood pounding in her ears. "One … two …."

"Wait. What about y—," she began.

"Three."

With a glare at her partner she yanked the door handle and propelled her body from the speeding Jeep. Before she jumped she thought she saw the slightest of smiles cross Benjamin Miller's lips. A trick of the light, she assured herself as her body flew from the speeding vehicle.

Hitting the concrete at 70 mph felt a lot like slamming into a brick wall. Sand, dust, and pavement bit into her flesh, ripping her bare skin to shreds. She tucked her arms over her head and rolled with the momentum, twisting and turning until she finally came to a stop, thirty feet from her initial leap, in the middle of the deserted roadway.

Through a haze of pain she managed to open her eyes. Her whole body felt like a side of ground beef. For a second she considered passing out, anything to avoid the waves of pain rolling over her shredded skin. Her limbs burned like hellfire under the hot desert sun.

Thankfully, after a few seconds the pain dulled to an intense throbbing and she was able to function. She rolled over on her stomach, wiping a stream of blood from her forehead. Her eyes scanned the surrounding roadway for any signs of her partner.

Finding none, she looked toward the runaway Jeep. A few hundred feet ahead of her, it barreled out of control and disappeared over a hilltop.

A flash of orange light filled the sky, followed by an explosion so loud it shook the desert, knocking Six from her feet. And then silence. Cold, deadly silence filled the heated air.

Chapter 4

〜

OPS Headquarters, Washington, DC
25May, 1000 hours

A WEEK LATER, IN a high-rise corner office in the center of downtown Washington, D.C., OPS Director Parker Langdon pored over the pages of the Bunny reports, weeding through every detail as if it held the secret to eternal life rather than disturbing details of death and destruction.

To the hundreds of people who passed daily by the headquarters of OPS, the building looked like a typical office complex. But it was anything but typical.

The CIA shell corporation, designed to protect capitalism at all costs, operated in a gray area, outsourcing trained CIA assassins to protect life, liberty, and the American way, as long as the American people never found out. That job—the secrecy part—fell into the hands of OPS Director Parker Langdon.

"What a mess," he said, dropping the file on his desk. Two assassins, his assassins, had nearly died last week, targeted by a bomb that sent a clear message. Not the kind of thing that looked good on one's résumé. Neither did the assassination of an innocent agent at the hands of one of his operatives.

Parker glanced down at the thick file in front of him. It read: MILLER, BENJAMIN. The file held thousands of pages of comprehensive reports on Miller's activities over the last five years of his employment with the agency. Each report read like an Ian Fleming Novel without the Briticisms. The sheer brilliance of each execution amazed the agent-in-charge.

Benjamin Miller was a dangerous man.

Parker glanced at another file, a lighter but just as terrifying read as the first.

His partner was pretty dangerous herself.

Maybe even more so.

Taking up the report sitting on his desk, he scanned the account of Davis Karter's murder, the one filled with the worst case scenario—a leak, a Judas among the ranks. A knock sounded at Parker's office door, pulling him from his dire thoughts. "Come in," he said.

The door opened, revealing an Asian woman in a tight black skirt. "Agent Miller is here, sir," the woman said, gesturing to the man looming behind her. Her eyes held blatant sexual appraisal as they swept over the assassin. Benjamin Miller, while one hell of a dangerous man, was also devastatingly handsome, with curly black hair a touch too long and messy, not to mention a dark, knowing smile that held promises he dared not keep.

"That will be all, Kim," Parker said. He frowned at his practically drooling executive assistant as he waved Ben into the spacious room. The two men, equally matched in size as well as intelligence, wordlessly shook hands.

Ben glanced about the room, noting the expensive rug and city view. *It's good to be the boss, especially on a government salary*, he thought, taking a seat across from Parker's polished desk. He stretched his legs out in front of him, wincing, as his muscles, still sore from the Jeep's explosion, pulled tight.

Ben studied Parker, weighing the meaning behind the

impromptu meeting. Like his office, Parker Langdon sparkled with wealth and privilege. His brown hair was streaked with blond highlights, as if the director had recently returned from a long holiday. The tie, slightly askew around Parker's neck, cost more than Ben made in a month. Oddly enough, Ben felt at home in his Levi's and Sonic Youth T-shirt, even in the opulent office.

"How are you?" Parker asked the killer in front of him.

Ben shot Parker a small smile. "Wondering why I'm here and not in the field. You've had me on lockdown for the last week. If this is about my injuries, the docs cleared me two days ago." The only outer reminder of Ben's near death experience was a slightly pink patch on his cheek and a sterile bandage around his left hand. Lucky to be alive, the docs said.

Ben didn't believe in luck.

Parker nodded. "I've reviewed your reports. The target, John Pillars—"

"Shouldn't we wait for Six?" Ben interrupted.

"Let's move forward without Ms. Winslow." Parker paused, his lips curling into a frown. "Tell me what you can about the incident. Did anything appear off about the target?"

"Other than the pink, fluffy bunny suit?"

Ignoring Ben's attempt at humor, Parker continued, "The report says you gave the order to take the shot."

"The GPS tracker authenticated the target. Six had a clean shot and I ordered her to take it."

"And an innocent man died," he said, "an agent from our very own agency. Does that strike you as odd?"

Ben's fist clenched against the arm of the chair and he took a steadying breath. "We followed your orders, based on the intel." Ben leaned forward, his eyes burning into the older man's. "If you want to pin this on someone, find whoever leaked our plan to John Pillars."

"I have," Parker said.

Ben leaned forward, his voice as cold as the Washington

winter. "Are you accusing me of something?"

Parker shook his head. "No."

"Then what's this about?" The assassin relaxed a little. "We followed our orders. Or is there something I'm missing?" Which wouldn't surprise Ben. As the offspring of a U.S. diplomat with ties to the CIA, Ben had been on a need-to-know basis since the day of his birth. Clandestine operations and lies, his daily bread. He hated it, hated not knowing who he could trust, so instead he trusted no one. Like father, like son.

"As you know, the man in the suit was not our target. His name was Davis Karter." Parker picked up a file from his desk and passed it over to Ben. "Karter was one of our agents working on special assignment. An assignment we believe got him killed."

Ben smiled, but without humor. Special assignment meant one thing. Karter was an agency snitch, a spy among spies. "How'd your guy end up in a desert wearing a bunny suit and strapped to a shitload of C-4?"

"We're not sure. The bomb destroyed any and all evidence." Parker paused, his face taking on a hard edge. "Davis was a good agent. A friend."

Ben tapped the dossier. "None of this explains why someone strapped a bomb to him."

Reclining in his high-backed chair, Parker stroked his chin with his long, tapered fingers. "True."

"So what now?" Ben rose from his seat and began to pace the plush carpet. His mind raced. Someone had planted that bomb in order to kill his partner and they'd nearly succeeded in killing three assassins for the price of one. That someone was John Pillars. "Is Pillars still our target?" Ben asked after a few minutes of silence.

Much to his surprise, Parker shook his head, a frown marring his features. "Not an active one. Thanks to this little screw-up." His eyes bore into Ben's. "Pillars has gone underground. Again. I've put Addison and Benson on him," he said referring to his number 2 assassination squad.

Ben hated both men, didn't trust them to get the job done—or any job for that matter. He'd seen their sloppy work firsthand. They were the type of assassins who got good people killed. He said as much as he slowly sat back down in the chair across from Parker. "You need us on Pillars. He's our target." A ghost target. OPS had little information on John Pillars. In fact, no one had seen the man's face. No one still breathing, that is.

"Not anymore." Parker banged his fist against his hardwood desk, rattling his BEST DIRECTOR coffee mug. Taking a deep breath, he straightened his desktop, as if stalling until he could regain control.

"What does that mean?" Ben said, his heartbeat accelerating. Something was very wrong. "We're off the case?"

Parker nodded once. "You are on paid leave until Internal Affairs finishes their investigation."

"Are you kidding me?" His voice grew colder. "We were doing our job. The job you hired us to do."

"Not quite," Parker said. The eyes that met Ben's were burning with fury. "IA believes Ms. Winslow has a new employer." His lips twisted with disgust. "An employer who paid her to sleep with Karter and eventually, after she got what they needed, kill him."

"That's crazy." Ben leapt from the chair, gulping back the lump that had formed in his throat.

Parker chose to ignore Ben's outburst, twisting the pen in his hand as he waited for the agent's anger to ease. "And then John Pillars tried to tie up loose ends by murdering Ms. Winslow. But he miscalculated, leaving his assassin alive. Now we finally have a chance to bring down his empire with the only person who has ever seen his face. As long as Hannah plays ball."

Ben gave a bitter laugh. "Six isn't a traitor. I know her, Parker. This isn't her."

Parker raised an eyebrow. "Then you know all about her relationship with Davis."

Frowning, Ben slowly slid back in his chair. As far as he knew, Six had never met the other agent. Hell, Ben had barely met the guy and he'd worked at OPS for five years. Assassins were rarely invited to company picnics or asked to play secret Santa.

Parker was far from finished. "Yes, a relationship—one that ended when she put a bullet in his head."

"It can't be," Ben whispered.

Parker's face hardened as did his voice. "Assassins have no loyalty." He paused, and a cold, hard smile spread across his face. "You know that better than anyone."

Chapter 5

~~

Six felt sick as she gazed down at the text message on her
iPhone for the tenth time.

One word had changed her life.

Forever.

"Danger," the mechanical type whispered in her head,
sounding almost demonic, if one believed in heaven and hell.
Six knew better. Hell was a place on Earth. She'd spent many
bloody days there, killing for her country.

A country that now wanted her dead.

She stared down at her phone once more, hoping it was all
some sort of mistake. But no, the word DANGER stared back.
She smiled, a grim expression that twisted her soft features
into hard lines and edges.

Two years ago, when she setup the early warning system in
case her file was ever flagged, Ben had called her paranoid. Not
paranoid, she'd told him, *prepared*. A girl, alone in the big bad
assassin world had to be ready for anything. At the time she
never expected that she'd have to use her escape plan.

Outwardly, the assassin showed no sign of her inner distress
as she started to pack up what little she needed from her

apartment, leaving behind white painted walls, dog-eared books, and a small television as well as some generic IKEA furnishings, all easily replaced. Like everything else in her life.

Or almost everything.

⊕

BEN GLANCED DOWN AT the cellphone vibrating in his pocket. Slowly, he lifted it from his jeans, careful not to draw Parker's gaze. Six's number flashed onto the screen. His finger hovered for a moment, heaviness filling his heart. Closing his eyes, he hit END, sending the call to voicemail.

Oblivious to Ben's distress, the director continued listing the OPS evidence against his partner. No, scratch that. His former partner. A woman, if Parker was right, he really never knew.

Parker said as much. "Aside from her relationship with Agent Karter, Ms. Winslow deposited a large sum of money in her bank account on the day of the assassination …."

Ben tuned Parker out as he continued to inventory Six's supposed sins. None of this mattered. When Six got here she'd clear all this mess up and they'd be back in the game. It was just a simple misunderstanding. A clerical glitch.

It had to be.

Why hadn't she told him about Karter? Had she been serious about him? Had she been in love? The thought enraged him, but he couldn't pinpoint why. Six was his partner. Her bed partners were none of his business. But why keep her relationship a secret? His fingers gripped the vibrating phone tighter. *Damn it, Six,* he thought. What else hadn't she shared with him?

His eyes fell to the small phone screen with the words, NEW VOICEMAIL, flashing on it.

Parker cleared his throat, drawing Ben's attention. "A team has been dispatched to bring Ms. Winslow in." He paused, overlapping his fingers.

"A team?" Ben asked, refocusing on the director. "What team?"

"Addison and Benson."

"I thought you were assigning them to John Pillars," he said. "Anyway, they won't find her. The address in her file is a fake." Like Ben's. Only two people besides Six knew where she really lived and one of them was dead. Ben pictured Six's small, Georgetown apartment with its girlie touches and cheap Swedish furniture.

"Where is she?"

Ben swallowed.

"Hannah must be brought in." Parker stared into Ben's eyes as if willing Six's location out of him. "Now. Today. Or more people will die." Parker sighed, leaning back in his chair. "I understand how hard this must be for you. And I'm sorry."

Ben gave a bitter little laugh. Fixing Parker with his eyes, his voice colder than the temperature-controlled room, he said, "Not as sorry as they will be when she sees them coming."

⊕

STANDING IN HER APARTMENT, packing years of her life into one suitcase, Six felt a deep sadness burning her throat. She thought of her family, mostly distant relatives scattered across the country, of her friends, not one who knew what she truly did for a living, and Ben. He would never understand her leaving. He would never forgive her either.

He was a soldier. The job was his life. It always had been. He knew nothing of love. Of friends or family. Ben Miller lived in a world of gray areas, but he saw only in black and white. Whatever he did, he did for a greater good, and that was enough for him.

She was nothing more than a number, the sixth in a line of partners. Ben's failure to answer her call proved as much. Her eyes cut to her iPhone, and Ben's number plastered across the redial screen. When she needed him most, he'd sent her to voicemail. For the first time in their three year partnership.

Message received. She was on her own.

She checked the clip of her 9mm.

Anger bubbled inside her, replacing the sick feeling in her stomach. Her life as she'd known it was over. And what hurt the most was, she would never know exactly why.

Maybe it was for the best. Time to move on. To become a real girl, one who found mister right and pushed out a brood full of kids, or barring that, one who owned a house full of cats. As an assassin she rarely thought about love. It just wasn't in the cards—too many lies and secrets for anything other than a fling.

But sometimes, late at night, she wanted more ….

Her mind flashed to Davis Karter, the divorced father of two, an agent with a quick smile and sweet disposition. A man she'd killed less than a week ago.

Tears filled her eyes as she remembered their last date. He'd taken her to an action movie where the hero saved the damsel in distress.

They'd shared popcorn.

He'd held her hand.

Afterward they'd walked through the quiet streets of Georgetown, passing people waiting for tables at the famous restaurants. They chatted about nothing important, just two people enjoying each other's company.

It was a fun night. Nothing too serious. Then Davis went from attentive to distant in a matter of seconds. When Six asked him what was wrong, he shrugged her question off. Years of training had her concerned nonetheless. At her apartment door he gave her a distracted kiss goodnight.

Six thought of inviting him in to see if there was any spark between them, but she was supposed to leave for a mission in Arizona early the next morning and Davis seemed preoccupied … or maybe he wasn't all that interested. Either way, she hadn't asked him inside. Instead, she kissed him on the lips and closed the door.

Three days later she shot him in the head.

Guilt nearly paralyzed her.

The slam of a car door in the street below forced her back to the here and now. She gazed down at the street. Two men sat in a gray sedan with darkly tinted windows. She could barely make out their shadows, but she knew their intent.

Ben had betrayed her. He'd given OPS her location.

And now two assassins were here to kill her.

She prayed Ben wasn't one of them.

Swallowing hard, she imagined the two of them facing off. One of them would die. Bile rose in her throat at the thought of taking Ben's life. Or any life, ever again.

Now was not the time for regrets and what ifs. Now was the time for action. Otherwise she would die. Here. And now. She rechecked the clip in her 9mm.

She didn't have much time, ten minutes tops, as the assassins were preparing to breech her statuary. They would check for exits, for hidden dangers, for the best way to end her life. And then they would come.

She yanked open the door of her freezer, pulling out a box labeled 'Frozen Enchilada Meal.' Inside was a passport in the name of Maria Gomez. Carefully she dug around the freezer for another box and another passport in the name of Sarah Jones. Two boxes later she had a total of four passports in various names with various pictures, all her but listing different weights, hair and eye colors.

Deeper inside the frozen tundra of her refrigerator she pulled out a box labeled 'Dove Bars' and dumped the contents onto the counter. There was a stack of bills, ten thousand dollars in all, as well as a chocolaty treat. As she pocketed the passports and cash, she bit into the rich ice cream, savoring the velvety goodness of what might just be her last meal.

Tossing the remains of her ice cream bar into the sink, she

picked up her cellphone, gazed at Ben's number one last time, and hit the delete button.

The screen went black.

Grabbing a bag filled with necessities, she opened the microwave, threw her cellphone inside with a bottle of oven cleaner, and plugged the appliance into a motion-activated outlet. With a grim smile she set the timer for thirty seconds.

⊕

PARKER SAT IN HIS high-backed chair with Hannah Winslow's file in his hand, his eyes on the assassin in front of him. Ben wasn't a believer. Not yet. But he would be soon. Too much evidence was mounting against his partner for his continued denial. Once she was brought in, the jig would be up, and Ben would see her for what she was—a cold-blooded killer. At least Parker hoped so. The stakes were too high for any other outcome.

The phone on Parker's desk let out a shrill ring, drawing the director's attention. He smiled, anticipating the imminent capture of Hannah Winslow.

"Don't do this," Ben said in warning.

Parker ignored him, punching the speaker button on the phone. "Langdon," he said to the caller.

"Director," Agent Benson said, the phone line crackling with static. "We are at the target's address."

Ben winced, again picturing Six's apartment, her ruffled couch cover, her retro funky lamps. The place smelled of lavender and other exotic fruity flavors. It fit her to a tee. The thought of Benson and Addison violating her space bothered him. His fingers curled around the arm of his chair, nearly cracking the delicately carved wood.

Parker glanced at the assassin opposite him, his eyes wary. "Do you have a visual on the target?"

"No, sir." The agent paused. "But thermal imaging detected one subject inside."

The director nodded. "Link to the video feed and proceed on my cue." As he said the words, a television screen on the other side of the office—a screen the size of a small country—flickered to life. Six's front door appeared on the video link.

Ben stood, his eyes passing from the screen to Parker. "Enough." He motioned to the phone. "Tell them to stand down."

"Sir?" Addison's voice crackled through the speaker.

Parker stared at Ben for a long minute. "Go."

Chapter 6

~~

Capital Apartments, Washington D.C.
25May, 1100 hours

AGENT GEORGE BENSON MOTIONED to his partner using two fingers to signal their advance. Frank Addison nodded in response. The two men had worked together for over ten years, knew each other's every move, like aging members of a boy-band who should've left the arena many years before. Both assassins knew something else as well. Hannah Winslow would come willingly or she would die. Her decision mattered little to either man.

At the doorway, for a brief second, fear skirted over Benson's senses. He'd heard the rumors, seen the evidence of her skills up close. Hannah Winslow was one hell of an assassin. She could kill at a thousand yards without breaking a sweat. He wiped the sweaty palm of his own gun-hand on his pressed pants.

Taking a deep breath, Benson gave his head a shake. What the fuck was wrong with him? Winslow was only one small female weighing a buck twenty at best. He outweighed her by a hundred pounds. Hell, he lifted one-twenty when he took a leak. He grinned at his own joke, mentally preparing to breech the door, his palms still a bit slick.

"Go," the director ordered in his ear.

With one last scan of the hallway he kicked the door as his partner tossed a flash grenade into Hannah Winslow's apartment.

$$\oplus$$

A BRIGHT FLASH OF white exploded across the television screen, momentarily blinding Ben. He blinked until his vision cleared. The sound of wood splintering filled the silent office as Benson and Addison breeched Six's inner sanctum.

Ben's heart slammed in his chest, but outwardly he showed no sign of distress. He wouldn't give Parker the satisfaction. Six's career, and maybe even her future existence, would be decided in the next few minutes.

$$\oplus$$

THREE BLOCKS AWAY, A woman with a METS cap riding low over her forehead walked with purpose down the street toward a storage complex. She looked neither right nor left, keeping her gaze straight ahead. Time was her enemy now. Well, time and the team of assassins bent on putting a bullet through her head. Assassins she'd once trusted with her life for a country she'd given up everything to protect.

Don't think about it, she ordered herself.

At the gates of U-Store she punched in a code she'd memorized long ago. The steel bars slowly creaked open, allowing her to make her way to unit 2B.

She glanced around and, finding nothing disturbed, she turned the wheels of the padlock until it popped open. Straining, she lifted the steel door. Dust rained down, causing a sneeze to bubble up inside her. "Ah-choo!" She waved her hand in front of her face to clear the air.

Once the dust settled, she smiled, her gaze settling on a 1995 Toyota Camry, silver in color, stored neatly inside the locker. Gassed up and ready to go.

Six pulled a Hide-a-key from the tire rim and opened the trunk. A briefcase sat inside, untouched, waiting for just this moment. She lifted the case from the car's confines, unlocked the driver's side door and slipped inside, placing the case on the seat next to her.

She started the vehicle, put it into gear, and drove through the parking lot, her face devoid of expression, a pair of sunglasses hiding the turmoil brewing behind the dark lenses.

For three years Six had lived in this friendly neighborhood, drunk coffee at Mr. Swenson's coffee shop, eaten dinner at the neighborhood hangouts—Joe's Pub and Wang's Chow House—shopped at Mr. G's, the mom and pop grocery store on the corner, and now, it was over.

She would never again wave at her next-door neighbor, Mr. Donahue, as he scooped up doggy-doo from his Pug, Shelia, or borrow a cup of sugar to make brownies (not that she ever made brownies, but it was the thought that counted) from Mrs. Frances in the apartment across the hall. Mrs. Frances had stopped by to borrow a candle during a power outage, once.

Swallowing hard, she took one hand off the steering wheel and popped open the briefcase. Inside lay an assortment of wigs and makeup, plus a lot of cash. Pocketing the cash, she left the wigs and makeup where they were for the moment.

Reaching deeper into the case, she pulled out a cheap, pay-as-you-go mobile phone with an emergency charger. She stared at the phone. She had no one to call for backup, not anymore. She was completely alone. Finally, with shaking hands and a heavy heart, she set the phone down on the seat next to her.

⊕

BENSON AND ADDISON BREECHED the room, guns at the ready. Thirty seconds later the microwave dinged. And blew apart, sending a cloud of thick chemical smoke into the air. Bits of microwaved flaming shrapnel flew about the kitchen, igniting the pale pink curtains above the sink.

As the oven exploded, both assassins hit the floor, sputtering and coughing as their lungs began to burn from the toxic smoke. They crawled out the door, glass and fried cellphone parts shredding their expensive pants.

Addison crawled to his knees and slowly stood, waving a hand in front of his face as he helped his singed partner to his feet. "Bitch almost killed us," he coughed.

Benson shook his head. Both men quickly assessed the damage surrounding them. The smoke, the fire, the shrapnel, nothing but bluster. "She knew what she was doing, that's for sure," Benson said as they made their way out of the apartment. He slammed the door shut behind them as the whoop of the building's fire alarms filled the hallway.

Parker watched the commotion from the safety of his desk chair, his expression growing colder with each blare of the alarm. After a minute, he turned to Ben, taking his measure. No show of surprise or happiness flickered in Ben's face. If anything, the assassin looked indifferent. "Six months," he said.

Parker turned to face him. The two men glared at each other. Parker broke the staring contest first, sighed, and returned to his seat. Silence filled the room.

"I can't authorize that." Parker shook his head, running a hand through his artfully arranged hair. "There are protocols. Procedures. Good God, when I think of the damage Winslow could do to the firm ...."

Ben leaned forward, his arms resting on the director's desk until the men were merely inches apart. "No one makes a move on her for six months." Six months would give Six enough time to settle in, to feel safe. And then he would have her.

And then he would have John Pillars.

And his mission would finally be complete.

"And if she kills more people while we're sitting on our asses? What then?" Parker crossed his hands over his chest as he leaned back in his chair.

"I'll deal with it." Ben paused, his next words echoing in the silent room. "With her."

Chapter 7

◦◦◦

THREE HOURS AFTER LEAVING everything behind, Six dyed her short pink hair light brown, changed her identity, and boarded a train for New York City.

In order to survive she had to disappear, to become someone new, in a whole new place. Thanks to a general lack of trust in her fellow man, OPS men in particular, Six had been planning for this eventuality for three years. A mistrust she'd learned from the very man who, in the end, was the worst Judas of all.

Ben mistrust bordered on paranoia, a trait she now embraced and which had served her well over the last week. But what Ben had taught her first and foremost was that to thrive in their world, she needed to be prepared for anything, especially an early retirement. Forced or not.

Over the next five days, Six changed her hairstyle twice, her identity four times, and plane-hopped to five different cities across the world, finally landing in LAX.

From there she 'borrowed' a Range Rover from the parking garage, drove it downtown and abandoned it in front of a sex shop. Exhausted and close to a total breakdown, she hopped a bus bound for San Diego.

Two hours later, she arrived at her new home, a comfortable condominium two blocks from the ocean, and her new life as Linda H. Burke, a recently divorced woman with a cat.

Six had never been fond of cats.

But she needed a fresh start, far from any connection to her old life. Or one day soon, two OPS assassins, much like Ben and herself—hell, maybe even Ben and his new partner—would arrive in town to remove their target. Until then she would try to forget about the past and make a new life for herself.

Easier said than done.

The buying part of getting a new life was relatively easy. Get a new social security number, a new ID, fake a few degrees, job experience, life experience, and bingo, a completely new woman was ready to face the world.

The cat was obtained through a cat rescue center. They were confused by her request: the most independent cat available. Age and breed were unimportant. The woman helping her made a few cracks. "You like a challenge, honey?" Six drove home with the optimistically named "Sweetie," the orneriest orange tabby cat this side of feral. Around ten years old. Sweetie wanted food and shelter, nothing touchy-feely for him. "That's fine, cat," she told Sweetie, refusing to use its name. "Keep to yourself, and you and I will get along just fine."

Sweetie kept his side of the bargain, escaping through the cat door whenever possible and returning only to eat and sleep—on every piece of furniture but her bed. Six, more alone than ever, spent the next week feeling the four walls of her unfurnished condo closing in. Sadness weighed heavily on her heart. Not only for the innocent life she had taken—the man she'd kissed goodnight—but also for her own identity. Hannah Winslow had loved working for OPS. It gave her a sense of pride, of accomplishment, of doing something for the greater good of the world.

Too bad it was all a lie.

The truth, the one that kept her locked away inside her

condo, was that Hannah Winslow no longer existed. She faded away the moment Davis Karter hit the dirt, leaving only the contract killer, Six, in her place.

A number with a bullet.

Six prayed Linda Burke would be more. Much more.

⊕

TWO WEEKS AFTER HANNAH Winslow escaped capture, the assistant director of OPS, Paul Fuller, looked at the missive in his hand and then at his boss. "There's still no sign of Winslow."

Parker ran a hand through his hair, frowning at the gray strand wound around his thumb after he pulled away. This mess with Hannah Winslow was taking its toll. Since she'd vanished into thin air, Parker had spent many nights lying awake, waiting for a phone call that would destroy his carefully constructed house of cards.

He glanced up from his computer screen, his eyes searching Fuller's blank features. "Put two more agents on it."

"But, sir, you swore to Agent Miller."

"What Agent Miller doesn't know …." Parker frowned. "How is Agent Miller getting along with his new partner?"

Paul shook his head. "He isn't."

⊕

DAYTIME TV WASN'T HELPING Six's self-imposed exile. *Judge Judy*, *Ellen*, and *Days of Our Lives* swirled around her all day long, proving what she already knew: she was a lousy specimen of womanhood.

Sweetie sometimes deigned to sleep on the chair next to the couch, looking up every so often as if to say, "You *enjoy* this garbage?"

Somehow Six's CIA training had missed the importance of the water bra, Brazilian waxes, and marrying your ex-husband's father to spite your twin sister, a woman with only a month to live. Six clicked off the TV and sighed. She needed to find a way out of this funk, and more importantly, she needed to stay away from daytime TV.

She needed a job. Something mindless. Something that didn't require bullets, bombs, or betraying partners. Just thinking about Ben made her angry all over again. For all his talk of partner loyalty and trust, when it came down to it, he'd sold her out. Six bet he actually believed the lies OPS fed him about her. By now he'd probably replaced her with a brand new partner. The thought turned her stomach, even as her heart squeezed with an unfamiliar longing.

She'd show him. She'd show all of them. Hannah Winslow was more than an easily expendable paid killer. More than a disposable number for Ben Miller's amusement.

Grabbing the *San Diego Union Tribune* off her neighbor's doorstep, she flipped to the classified ads and scanned the rows of job listings, searching for the perfect match. Administrative Assistant? She shook her head. She could barely type forty words per minute, and she despised making coffee. Plus, the pay sucked.

C.P.A.?

Again she shook her head. The only accounting she'd ever done was body counts and she doubted that qualified her for tax season. Her job prospects looked bleak. *You're a smart, confident woman*, she reminded herself. How hard could it be to find a job?

Sadly, it turned out to be harder than CIA training camp.

By the second week of job hunting, she'd busted two pairs of expensive heels and broken three nails during an onsite typing test as well as three ribs. Not her own ribs, but those of a potential employer—a jerk whose idea of an interview involved a lot of groping and an ill-placed kiss.

Sick of job hunting, interviews, and herself, Six decided to approach her quest for a career as she would an assassination target. She spent the next week gathering intel. She spent hours scouring the web for the right target, a job with the right balance of pay, benefits, and tedium. A career that would fit her new persona, Linda H. Burke, to a T.

Once she zeroed in on a profession, she started to network with the headhunters—the business kind, not the assassin type. Oddly enough, the former seemed much more blood-thirsty.

Armed with her weapons of choice—a fake résumé, a black briefcase filled with files rather than knives, and a gray pin-striped suit fresh off the JCPenny's sale rack—she went to interview for the perfect job to begin her new life.

An hour later, Zachary Coleman Barber, the owner of H2, an up-and-coming bottled beverage company, glanced up from her bogus references and smiled. "When can you start?"

Six relaxed a bit, allowing the first real smile since leaving OPS to cross her lips. "Right away," said the new marketing manager of a company that offered good pay, flexible hours, health, dental, as well as a 401(k). And, as an added bonus, she didn't have to kill anyone to get it.

Or so she hoped.

Chapter 8

~~~

Sunny Side Condominiums, San Diego, CA
28 Jun, 1800 hours

SIX CLIMBED THE STAIRS to her condominium, a bouquet of daisies and a cup of coffee in her hands. She'd done it. She'd gotten the job, a real nine-to-five, no bloodshed or fear of death, kind of job. Things were looking up. For the first time in six weeks, her heart became a little less heavy.

Tomorrow morning Linda Burke would begin her life. She'd make friends. Go out for drinks with her co-workers. Laugh at the boss' jokes. Maybe she'd meet Mr. Right or a reasonable facsimile. They could fall in love, get married, and have a brood of kids.

Sweetie meowed inconclusively. His food dish was full and his litter box empty, so perhaps he was offering congratulations.

The very thought of embracing domesticity scared the hell out of the once deadly assassin. She decided right then she'd rather take a bullet.

Sweetie brushed against her legs. She reached down to pet him, but he had already disappeared through the cat door.

⊕

OPS Headquarters, Washington, D.C.
20Sept, 1200 hours

"FUCK. YOU SHOT ME," Ben yelled, reaching for his shoulder to staunch the river of blood ruining his beloved Ramones T-shirt.

The man in front of him, more of a kid really, glanced down at the 9mm on the floor and then to his blood-covered new partner. The kid's already pale face turned two shades whiter. "I'm so sorry, sir. It was an accident. The gun fell and …."

Ben closed his eyes and counted to ten and then twenty before speaking. "Call the medic."

"On their way," Paul Fuller, Ben's long-time friend and mentor said from the doorway of the shooting range. "Son," he said to the kid, "why don't you wait for them in the hall?"

The kid did as ordered, practically running from the blood splattered room. Ben stared after him, slowly shaking his head. "Thanks," he said.

Paul flashed a bright smile. "I didn't do it for you. Ten more seconds and you'd have killed him." He let out a drawn out sigh. "And you know how much I hate all that paperwork."

Ben shrugged. Paul was probably right. He was so tired of screw-ups, of new partners with no skills or brains. For the past five months he'd suffered through partner after partner— Special Forces drones, Army Rangers, Navy Seals, and plain old psychos.

Some lasted a few weeks, others only a couple of days before Ben finally snapped. He'd busted the first guy's arm and the second one's front teeth. Much to his dismay, the third one managed to escape before any violence had been perpetrated.

His latest partner, Curtis Daniels, or 'Ten,' as Ben referred to him, had just graduated from CIA training camp, top of his class, after a four-year stint in the Army Rangers. His second day as an OPS operative and he'd shot his boss.

Not a great start.

Ben had to give the kid credit, though. He'd lasted longer than the last one, Nine, had. Still, getting shot sucked. A wave of dizziness punctuated his thoughts. Holding his shoulder, he slid down the cement wall and onto the floor, leaving a smear of blood.

"Kid's got shitty aim," Paul said, eyeing the wound.

Ben closed his eyes and nodded.

"You look like hell." Paul's voice rose with concern. "How bad is it?"

"Through and through." He opened one eye. "Hurts like a bitch."

"Good," Paul said, taking a seat on the floor next to Ben, careful not to wrinkle his thousand-dollar suit or muse his perfectly styled salt and pepper hair. Appearance meant a lot to Paul, the only flaw Ben saw in his otherwise faultless friend, the man who taught him everything he knew about being an assassin. Center mags, Paul had told Ben time and again. Always shoot for the center of the chest.

Paul was saying, "What's going on with you? You walk around like a wounded bear, clawing at anyone who crosses your path. You've been through three partners in five months. The last one lasted a day."

Ben snorted.

"Is it Hannah?" Paul stared at Ben as if searching for any sign of weakness. "It's September, five months since she left. Not a blip on any radar." He paused. "She hasn't been in contact with you, has she?"

Ben shook his head, grinning through the pain radiating down his arm. He'd taught her well. Even with Parker's promise to leave her be—a vow he'd broken two days after making it—in the last five months of searching for Six, OPS had come up with nothing. At least according to his sources. They'd tracked her as far as Paris.

In another couple of weeks it would be Ben's turn to find her, a task he dreaded as much as meeting the next inept and aggravating partner OPS assigned him.

His orders were clear.

His mission: bring Hannah Winslow in alive. But first, Ben had other plans for his former partner.

"You could let her go. Forget the whole investigation." Paul lowered his voice to a whisper in case Big Brother decided to listen in on their conversation.

Ben shook his head. "Can't."

Paul patted Ben's good arm. "Trust me, my friend, the truth you desperately want—the truth about Hannah, about what happened in Arizona—will come with a price. One I hope you won't pay with your life."

Ben rubbed his chin with his good arm. Paul would never understand his need to find Six. It was much more than personal; it was an obsession. He needed to know if their relationship had been just a lie, even if it cost him his life. The thought of Six betraying him ate at what was left of his soul. He stayed up nights picturing her slightly crooked smile, wondering if it was a ruse, if the corner of her lips had curved up in that unforgettable smirk while she'd plotted to destroy him.

On the day Six left, he'd sat in Parker's office intent on aiding her escape by demanding a six-month moratorium. He wanted to give her time to disappear, to stay safe.

As the days passed, a jumble of doubts rocked the normally cold assassin. The evidence against his former partner was mounting. Handwritten notes detailed a fiery love affair between Six and Karter. Wire transfers from an account in Grand Cayman to a secret account in Six's name. Photographs. Emails. Burner cellphones. All these things added up, forcing Ben to face the possibility that Six wasn't the woman he'd thought she was.

Each passing week only increased his agitation. John Pillars stayed underground, out of sight, leaving OPS to focus on building a case against Six. A strong case too.

Every day she spent out in the cold was filled with peril. OPS wouldn't be the only ones searching for the runaway assassin. Sanctioned killers like Six had a way of picking up enemies, and those enemies could smell fresh blood in the water from hundreds of miles away. Not to mention the fact that John Pillars wanted her dead, and he was more than willing to kill anyone in his way.

"Fine," Paul said, dragging Ben back to the present. "If you're so intent on bringing her in, why not go today? What are you waiting for? Take Curtis to watch your back and go find her."

How could he explain to Paul what he could barely justify to himself? A small part of him still wanted Six to be free, to have the life she said she wanted, a life that he himself would never have. A life away from death. Away from killers like him. Yet, there was a bigger reason. One he wouldn't share with anyone. Not until the time was right. And all the pieces fell into place.

"Watch your back." Paul straightened as two medics in dull green scrubs pushed into the room. "If you get in Pillars' way, he will kill you." Paul's dire words rang in Ben's ears long after the medics loaded him onto the waiting gurney and took him away.

Chapter 9

~

Halekulani Resort, Honolulu, HI
25Oct, 1400 hours

Linda H. Burke smiled at the dark-skinned bartender and ordered another round. "Tequila. Neat."

The man poured her drink, flirting with the russet-haired beauty in front of him as the warm Hawaiian sun bronzed their skin. "What brings you to paradise, sweetheart?" he asked with a wicked smile. "Business or pleasure?"

"Maybe a little of both," Linda said with her own impish and slightly crooked grin. She tossed down a ten dollar bill. In her wildest dreams, Linda could have never imagined a place as perfect to relax and regroup as the Halekulani Resort in Honolulu.

Of course, her alter ego, Six, knew perfection and it wasn't to be found at a five-star hotel. *Almost paradise*, she thought, reaching for the Tequila shooter. Take away the warm island winds, cute Polynesian bartenders, and the smell of roasting pig for tonight's Luau, and all that was left was a group of drunken executives and their high-maintenance mistresses. A fun crowd for a night, but after three days you needed a long, hot shower. And some bleach.

Today was day four.

"Linda. Come over here," a man in Bermuda shorts and a flowery shirt called from across the bar. Six took a large swallow of tequila, plastered a serene yet clueless 'Linda' smile on her face, and strolled over as if she was having the time of her life.

"Hi, Zach. I'm really looking forward to the Luau tonight," she said to her boss and the owner of H2 Enterprises.

Zachary Coleman Barber pulled out a chair for his marketing director. "Have a seat. Can I get you another drink?" He nodded to her half-empty glass.

She shook her head. When you spent your life looking over your shoulder, partying could be fatal, and she wasn't the kind of girl to make that mistake. Sex, drugs, and rock-n-roll were for those without targets on their backs.

"The sales figures are up for next quarter," she said when the silence between them lengthened. He grinned, flashing perfect teeth. Like everything else on Zach.

He was a beautiful specimen of manhood, from his wavy, highlighted blond hair to his buff but not overly muscular body. Rich, good-looking, single, and yet, he seemed like the average boy next door. The women in the office adored him. Surprisingly not a whiff of office scandal surrounded him.

He waved to the bartender for another drink. "Relax, Linda. H2 is thousands of miles away. It's time to enjoy all that great work you've done for the last four months." He raised his drink in salute, condensation dripping down the side of the glass. "To the victor goes the spoil."

She mimicked his salute with her own glass.

"What are your plans for the rest of the day?" he asked, running a hand through his sun-drenched hair. "Dip in the pool? Hot stone massage?" He shook his head. "Nope, that's not it. You strike me as more the adventuress type." He leaned in, his breath warm against her bare shoulders. "What do you say to," he paused, drawing out his next words like a caress, "a hike up the volcano? It was off-limits to tourists for years. Care to live on the edge with me?"

Six glanced around his wide shoulder to the sleeping volcano ridge bursting above the tree line. A rocky slope trailed up the side. For the first time in six months, true excitement surged through her, whether from the prospect of a dangerous hike or the man next to her, she wasn't sure. Either way, she was glad to finally feel something besides the mind-numbing boredom of the last six months.

Her gaze flicked over the perfect male specimen in the form of her boss. The next couple of hours with Zach would be anything but monotonous, and it was about time. Six was dying for some excitement. If she'd learned anything in the last six months, it was that being Linda H. Burke was beyond dull.

No wonder she owned a cat. She thought about Sweetie, the world's most independent cat. She had hired their receptionist, who happened to live nearby, to come in twice a day to clean the litter box and fill the food dish. She had recently purchased one of those little fountains as a water dish, to simulate running water. She had even found herself giving Sweetie a few strokes now and then. Damn cat.

⊕

THE HIKE UP DIAMOND Head, once the most active Hawaiian volcano, took about two hours along a worn and twisting path overgrown with vegetation. Tropical flowers burst from the humid volcanic atmosphere in a nearly blinding explosion of color.

An hour into the hike, Six started to believe in paradise. Everything was so beautiful, almost perfect. When Zach took her hand it seemed like the most natural act in the world. Linda Burke was finally living the way destiny had intended.

Hand in hand, the pair climbed higher into the sky. She imagined the smell of sulfur from the volcano's active past, and as she did, the excitement in her belly grew. Something was happening. Something amazing. Her imagination went wild, allowing her to feel a rumble under her feet, a warning of danger perhaps, though easily ignored.

"So you grew up in Grand Rapids?" Zach asked, his hand warm in hers.

"Right outside the city. On a farm," she improvised, which was dangerous in itself, the excitement of the day making her a bit reckless. "And you?" She squeezed his hand. "Where do you call home?"

"Originally, D.C."

At the mention of her former hometown her stomach clenched. Was Zach connected to OPS? Was he somehow setting her up? Coldness pooled in the small of her back even in the sweltering humidity of the tropical paradise.

Her eyes searched his face for any signs of betrayal or deceit. Finding none, she relaxed slightly, shaking her head at her own paranoia. Zach was nothing more than a frat boy turned surfing CEO. She couldn't picture him with a weapon, let alone the cold calculation needed to kill. Briefly she recalled the hard glint in Ben's steely eyes.

"I moved after college," he said, bringing her back to the present. He smiled, his eyes intent on the riot of colors on the horizon. "San Diego will always be my home though. Nothing like waking up at dawn to surf and then heading in to the office."

She smiled, liking this man in front of her. He was smart, funny, self-deprecating, and gorgeous. 'Linda' could fall for him. It would be so easy. One little kiss. As in a fairytale, he could turn her into a real girl instead of a number.

A branch cracked nearby. She spun to face the danger, her fantasy vanishing in a wink. When nothing appeared from the brush, her heartbeat slowly returned to normal.

"Must be a bird," he said with a laugh. "Don't tell me my fearless marketing director is scared of a little birdy. Why, I've seen you facedown even the most daunting of ad copy."

The way he said the words should've been charming, but to Six, they sounded almost patronizing. Damn, there went her fairytale life. Rather than tell him off, Linda gave a flirty squeal, much to Six's dismay. She batted her eyelashes. "What if it wasn't a bird, but a big, bad wolf?"

"My, what big teeth you have." He smiled wider, pulling her into his muscular arms. He smelled of soap and man, and for a second, she allowed herself to feel the rush of chemical attraction. It had been so long since any man had touched her.

Not since Davis ….

His hands slid up her shoulders, pausing at the curve of her neck, pulling her into a kiss. Their lips met, softly at first. Not bad, she thought seconds before his tongue swept into her mouth. The kiss deepened, growing hotter as lava pulsed underneath their feet. Heat pooled low in her stomach. She wrapped her leg around his thigh, increasing the reckless energy between them.

It felt so good to be held, to feel the touch of another human being without questioning his motives. She wanted this feeling to last forever, to unfreeze the coldness locked in her heart. A coldness left by Davis' death and Ben's betrayal. The pain, anger, and sadness surrounding her feelings for Ben quickly cooled her ardor as she pictured her former partner and compared the man who held her in his arms to a man she might never forget or forgive.

Zach broke the kiss, his breath coming in short gasps. "Wow … umm … I—"

Gunfire cracked.

Bits of bark from the tree next to the couple exploded, sending toothpick-sized shards into her skin. Acting on pure instinct, she wrapped her arms around Zach and dove off the steep rocky cliff.

Chapter 10

"**O**H, SWEETIE, ARE YOU all right?" Helen Smith, Six's friend and co-worker at H2, asked as Zach carried Six into the lobby of the opulent resort. His thousand dollar hiking boots squeaked on the polished marble floor.

For a moment Six thought Helen was referring to her cat.

"She'll be fine," he said, giving Six a light squeeze. A leaf fell from her mused hair. "Just a couple of scratches. Nothing that won't heal. She'll be back to her beautiful self in no time."

Helen's eyes widened as she looked from Six to Zach and back again. Her cheeks turned a slight pink and so did Six's. From the look of Zach and her disheveled appearance, Six could only imagine the thoughts racing through Helen's head. "I tripped," she blurted. "Zach saved me." A lie, but why not make Zach feel like a hero? He had carried her halfway down a mountain, after all. A bone of contention since she felt perfectly capable of walking, slightly sprained ankle aside. But Zach insisted. Yet another strike against the blond Adonis.

"You could have been killed!" Helen's hand flew to her mouth. Tendency toward dramatics aside, Six liked Helen. The divorced mother of two had guts and determination, not to mention a wardrobe in every array of brown imaginable. In Six's opinion, that outweighed her occasional hysterics.

Six smiled at Helen's concern. "Really. I'm fine. A hot shower and I'll be good as new." Another lie, but she doubted Helen would appreciate the truth. She would not be *good* again, not until the assassin lurking in the bushes was dead. The killer had taken a risk on the volcano top. A risk she would make sure came back to haunt him.

"Let's get you upstairs," Zach said, shifting her in his arms as if she weighed nothing. "To bed," he added in a whisper. A shiver passed through Six, but not of lust. She felt the killer's eyes on her, felt him waiting for a chance to pounce.

She'd known since the day she'd left D.C. that this day would come. Time to pay for past sins.

Not all of them her own.

$\oplus$

FOUR HOURS LATER, FRESHLY showered, bandaged, and armed with multiple weapons, Six wrapped a piece of carpet fiber around the handle of her door and closed it behind her. If when she returned, the fiber was gone, she'd know the killer waited inside her suite.

That would be his final mistake.

With one final glance at the doorknob, she headed down the hallway to the elevators. Four stories below, Zach and the rest of the H2 executives waited for her at the tiki bar next to the luau.

Tonight promised to be something; she just wasn't sure what. Her co-workers knew how to party and they took great pleasure in the process. Six gazed down at her red sundress, debating its ability to withstand fruity drink stains as well as conceal the Kel-Tec P32 pistol tucked in a holster on her thigh. The gun was small, but it could pack a punch at close range. As much as she hated the thought of using the weapon, or any weapon ever again, she wasn't ready to die.

She wore her dark hair twisted up into a stylish updo and a touch of gloss on her lips. While she appeared the height of fashion, her guiding force was the ability to act and react to any situation. Not for the first time in the last few months did she miss her short hairstyle and combat boots.

Too often she'd seen women fall prey to violence due to their accessories. A simple necklace became a noose in the right hands. A pair of high heels were just as dangerous, a fact she was counting on tonight. Let the assassin make the mistake of underestimating her. It might be the only advantage she had.

The elevator dinged a floor above the lobby. Six stepped off and walked down the remaining flight of stairs, her shoes tapping against the concrete steps.

No reason to make killing her easier. Killer's Rulebook 101—assassins relied on rituals, those pesky little habits people acquired over time such as driving the same route to work, stopping at the same Starbucks at lunch, or parking in the same spot in the office lot. Predictable behavior made killing a person simpler, and she wasn't about to let a minor thing like getting off the elevator at the right floor end her life.

With ease she'd stepped back into the watchful role she had abandoned nearly six months ago. Her CIA training was part of it, but what she'd learned from Ben was even more valuable.

Never trust anyone.

Apparently that truth extended to partners as well.

Eyes alight and watchful, she made her way into the bustling lobby of the resort. She watched the crowd for anyone showing too much interest in her arrival, her search fueled not by vanity but years of survival skills.

The air smelled of exotic flowers and roasted pig with a hint of salty ocean air. Toward the back of the tiki bar crowded with sunburned tourists, half-obscured by a large orange umbrella, sat Zach and the rest of the H2 crew. Judging by the amount of empty glassware and plastic swords on the table, they'd been there for a while.

Zach waved her over. She waved back, carefully wending her way through the crowd. The closer she got to the group, the more she relaxed. The odds of the assassin making his move in a crowded hotel were slim. Plus, Zach looked gorgeous in a black sports coat and jeans, his blond hair spiked in just the right directions. At least she'd have something nice to look at during what promised to be another lame team-building dinner/drink-a-thon.

She sighed, wishing she could feel more for Zach. It would make things so much easier. As if reading her mind, Helen caught her gaze and smiled. Six grinned back, surprised she'd noticed the middle-aged CPA at all. Helen's brown dress was a perfect match for her brown hair and the dark wood paneling inside the bar.

On Helen's right, Ron Jazz, Human Resources Manager, groped his administrative assistant, a buxom redhead named Charlotte. Ron's mousy wife, Christie, sat across from Ron pretending not to notice. A couple more executives rounded out the group. Their faces gleamed an unhealthy shade of red from sunburn and alcohol.

She scanned the rest of the crowd, expecting the telltale ping of adrenaline to warn of any danger. Finding none she let out a pent-up breath and sat in the empty chair next to Zach.

"There you are," he said, leaning in to kiss her cheek. He smelled of alcohol and pine cologne—not a bad scent, like a visit home for Christmas. She blushed, because really, that's what her co-workers would expect Linda Burke to do.

"Hi," she said.

"Feeling better?"

"Tip-top," she responded. Who used the words 'tip-top'? What did Zach see in Linda? Boobs, she thought, given the number of glances he snuck at her chest.

Oh, the miracle of the water bra.

"Can I get you a drink?" he asked her breasts.

"Chardonnay, please."

Zach flagged down a passing waiter and gave him her order. Her drink arrived promptly, cold and sparkling in the dim hotel bar light. She pretended to take a sip, swirling the liquid around the crystal glass. The warm trade winds off the ocean filled her senses and she relaxed a bit more. The weight of her weapon and the scent of the salty waters washed away her uneasiness.

"Beautiful, isn't it?" Zach said, staring intently into her eyes. A swell of something stirred within her, not quite desire but *something*. Maybe she should take the chance. Zach was everything she should want in a man. He was good-looking, smart, and owned his own business. So why didn't he turn her on? What was wrong with her? In the back of her mind, Ben's face swirled around.

As if she'd conjured him up from the depths of assassin hell, a familiar voice said, "Linda? Linda Burke? Is that really you?"

Her stomach lunged into her throat and she turned to face certain death. She blinked a few times in disbelief. How the hell had he found her? She'd covered her tracks well.

Apparently not well enough. Ben stood before her, looking hot and deadly in a dark blue suit, his black hair slicked back from his handsome face. *Who died?* she wanted to ask, eyeing his funereal suit, but decided she probably wouldn't like his answer.

"I'm sorry." She tilted her head to the side, hating the way her heart lurched at the sight of him. "Do I know you?"

Ben blinked, full of innocence, a smile spreading across his face. "It's me. Ben Miller. From East Grand Rapids High. Go Cougars!" He pumped his fist in the air, an action that made her consider stabbing him with her wine glass. He seemed to recognize the look in her eye, for he stepped out of striking distance before adding, "Don't tell me you forgot me already?"

"Doesn't ring any bells," she answered, lips frozen in a stiff smile, heart thundering in her chest. Beads of sweat pooled between her breasts as her body fought its natural fight or flight response. *Run*, her mind screamed, but her assassin's heart stayed deadly calm.

"Really?" He frowned, acting for all the world like the boy next door, when in truth, he was the last man anyone in their right mind wanted showing up at their door. "I sat next to you in biology senior year. Mr. Banks' class." He bent his head in an 'aw shucks' way. "I asked you to prom."

Ben knew damn well she never graduated high school, went to prom, or did any of those teenage things. Due to her intelligence and unique skills with firearms, the CIA had recruited her at fifteen and immediately started her training. High school forgotten. On the other hand, Linda Burke proudly displayed her East Grand Rapids diploma on a desk in her San Diego condo.

Damn him.

She felt violated, picturing him pawing through her, or rather Linda's, most intimate personal effects. She only prayed he hadn't opened her third dresser drawer ....

"Oh." Six affected a blush, one that felt very real as it crawled up her cheeks. "That's right. You were in the chess club. Wore those big, black glasses."

He grinned, tapping his eyelids with his trigger finger. "Lasik. Still play a mean Pawn's Game though."

Helen clapped her hands together. "How lovely. Imagine, your very own high school reunion. What're the odds?"

"Yes," Six said. "What are the odds?"

"I'd say they're pretty good." Ben gave a laugh, a sound that grated as it filled her with longing, much to his delight—if the sparkle in his eyes could be trusted.

She felt the blood leave her face. "Excuse me for a minute."

"Of course," he said. "Hurry back. I'm looking forward to catching up. After all, we have so much time to make up."

With a curt nod, she rose from her barstool, palmed her

pistol, and strolled toward the restroom as if she didn't have a care in the world. Inside, her heart pounded with equal parts fear, sadness, and rage. How dare Ben be the one OPS sent to kill her? She'd saved his ass a time or two. Wasn't that worth anything to the cold-blooded bastard?

At least one question was answered. The assassin from this afternoon, the one who tried to murder her, was her ex-partner. Oddly she'd never known him to miss a target, not at such close range and with such a clean shot. Not that it mattered. He wouldn't miss a second time.

So what was his endgame? Why show himself now? Was he toying with her? A year ago she would've sworn he didn't have it in him.

The bastard.

He'd already betrayed her. Now he would try and kill her. She took a deep breath, checked her makeup in the mirror, and fingered the safety on her weapon. The cold metal calmed her somewhat. Ben was a professional. He wasn't about to shoot it out in the middle of a luau.

She hoped.

Pushing through the bathroom door she tumbled into the arms of a younger man. He couldn't be more than twenty-two by the look of his unlined face.

"Sorry, ma'am," Curtis Daniels, or rather 'Ten' said, steadying her. His smile appeared sincere, but the hairs on her neck rose.

"No problem," she answered, pushing from the stranger's arms and heading back into lair of the lion.

Chapter 11

~~

"**S**HE WAS THE ONE that got away," Ben was saying when Six returned to the table. He sat next to Helen, a frosted bottle of beer in his hand. He punctuated his statement with a little wave salute in Six's direction. "I swore that if I got another chance I wouldn't let her get away a second time." He tilted the bottle toward her like a weapon. "Ever."

Instead of creeping her co-workers out, he was keeping them fascinated by dangling an unfolding 'love' story before their very eyes. Everyone except Zach; he just looked pissed. His forehead wrinkled and a frown marred his gorgeous face.

"That's very sweet," Six said, the tone of her voice suggesting it was anything but. "But it's been a long time. Surely you've moved on."

"Oh, I've tried." He smiled at Helen. "But ... *Linda* will always be my ... first love." The humor in his eyes fed her rage. He was playing with her. Toying with her like Sweetie did with any passing mouse. Well, *she* had claws too, and she damn well knew how to use them.

"So tell me," Ben said, breaking into her dark thoughts, "what have you been up to?"

"This and that," she said.

The kindhearted Helen answered for her, "Linda works with us at H2 in San Diego. She's the head of our marketing department."

"Smart *and* beautiful. That's my girl," Zach said, wrapping a possessive arm around Six's shoulders. Ben's smile tightened, but he merely nodded. Six, on the other hand, wanted to punch Zach in his perfect nose. She wasn't *anyone's* girl.

"Zach," Helen indicated her boss, "decided we needed a break so he popped for this team building trip. The resort is wonderful. I never want to leave."

As opposed to Six, who wanted to disappear right now. The tension at the table increased with each testosterone filled moment. Zach glared at Ben, who seemed oblivious, but she knew better. Butter knives at dawn perhaps?

"And what is it you do?" Zach asked.

"Well," Ben grinned, "I killed the president of Paraguay with a fork." Six's indrawn breath drew a laugh from her ex-partner as the rest of the group started to giggle.

Helen clapped her hands. "*Grosse Point Blank*. I love that movie."

Movie? Six glanced at Ben—she clearly remembered an assassination in Paraguay involving stemware—but her ex-partner's face remained impassive. She shivered under the starry sky.

The luau hostess arrived at their table, breaking up the gabfest. "We are ready for you now. Please come this way." She motioned outside the resort's lobby to a sandy, paved beach and a twirling pig on a spit surrounded by rows of beauties with tropical flowers in their hair. Six felt sorrier than usual for the pig.

"Well," Ben rose, "it's been a real pleasure, but I'll leave you to your meal."

"Nice to meet you," Helen said, her face flushed. "I hope we'll see you again soon."

"You will," he said, eyes intent on Six. "That's a promise."

⊕

THE WALK TO HER hotel room later that evening was the longest of Six's life. She jumped at every shadow. Ben was close. She could practically smell his scent, a combination of testosterone and bad-ass.

Sick of men, Ben in particular, she was thankful when Zach had taken her hint. The slight bulge in his pants when he walked her to the elevator told her exactly what he wanted. But she declined, giving him a chaste kiss on the cheek as she stepped inside the elevator. Alone. No reason to get them both killed.

She rode the elevator to the third floor and took the stairs the rest of the way to her room, keeping to the shadows. A couple of doors from her goal, she saw a door swing open. Out stepped the young man she'd run into at the bar.

While she believed in many things, alien life for example, she doubted this man just happened to book the room next to hers.

The young man looked surprised by her appearance, his eyes widening at the sight of her. He was even more surprised when she kicked his door closed and slammed him against the wall. Her gun dug into his sternum. "Who are you?" she asked, slipping off the safety.

"Curtis ... Daniels ... m-ma'am," he stammered.

"Who do you work for, Curtis?" Her voice went soft and warm as if the topic was as insignificant as the weather. When he didn't answer fast enough to suit her, she pressed the barrel deeper into his chest, causing him to whimper. Rather than self-satisfied, she felt ill as the image of Davis' blood-smeared face flashed through her mind.

"Let him go," Ben whispered from behind, the cold steel of his weapon caressing the back of her neck. "Now, Six," he added when she hesitated, "you're not *that* fast."

She released Curtis and slowly turned to face Ben, her gun leveled at his head.

His was aimed at her heart.

Chapter 12

~

"TEN," BEN SAID, HIS voice deadly calm, "if she pulls the trigger, put two in the back of her head."

"Yes, sir," Curtis said.

Six smiled. "Who's your green friend?"

"Ten. Army Ranger," Ben said as if that explained Ten's lack of skills and puppy-dog eagerness. After all, a girl took him down before he could even cock his gun. Of course Six wasn't just any girl. She was a trained killer.

And a traitor.

Ben weighed his options. Shooting Six in the middle of a hotel filled with rich people held little appeal. On the other hand, being shot twice in a month wasn't his fondest wish either.

"I see," she said as if weighing her own options.

Ben could see her brain working. She would get the drop on him. Take the kid out. Freedom. Kill him. Here and now. Ben's heart rate hit 120 but his hand stayed steady.

Much to his surprise she lowered her gun. "How'd you find me?"

His heartbeat slowed to a semi-normal level, and he lowered

his own weapon, picturing the last few weeks of searching for her. "Wasn't hard," he lied, hating the fact he'd spent every dime of his expense account, contacted every informant he knew, and paid off half the degenerates and dirt bags on the coast and still turned up empty.

Until he remembered how much she hated southern California. From there, narrowing the search was a little easier, and within a week he had a location—sunny San Diego and the name Linda H. Burke.

"Did you really think I wouldn't find you?" He shook his head slowly. "That I'd let you get away with murder?"

Flinching ever so slightly, she motioned to her hotel room door. "Let's take this somewhere more private." Ben nodded, following her as she slid her keycard into the lock. The light flickered green and she pushed into the room.

"Wait here," Ben said to the younger assassin. "Don't let anyone interrupt us."

Once inside the room, she walked over to the bed and sat down, keeping her weapon in hand but kicking off her shoes. Ben smiled at the chaos. Clothes hung from the backs of chairs and books littered the floor. If he didn't know her better he'd have called the cops to report a burglary. "You haven't changed much," he said, smiling over the mess and the pink polish gracing her toenails. He'd missed her. Missed her chaos. Missed her slightly crooked smile. His life wasn't the same without her in it. Not that he'd admit it to her. He'd rather take two to the head.

"You've changed."

The edge in her voice caught him off guard. What the hell did that mean? "I missed you," he admitted grudgingly.

"So I noticed."

What was going on here? Six's cold rage wasn't making any sense. Ben expected mistrust, but not full-on insanity. Crazy wasn't Six. She was levelheaded and too smart—not to mention sexy as hell—for her own good.

She let out a loud sigh. "Let's just get this over with."

"Get what over with exactly?"

Her forehead wrinkled. "The killing."

"Killing?" He frowned. "What killing?"

"You're not here to kill me?"

Ben couldn't help it, he laughed. Big, loud guffaws at her expense which, from the darkening of her sapphire-colored eyes, was making her want to kill him for the hell of it.

She shot him a frown. "You want me to believe that you're not here to kill me? That you're on some kind of vacation and just happened to run into me?"

"Not quite."

"If it's not murder on your mind, why are you here?" Her voice sounded suspicious to his ears.

"Like I said." Ben took a step toward her, hating the flash of fear he detected in her gaze. Fear that she quickly masked. "I missed you, Six. Come back to D.C. I promise I'll make things right with Parker. You can have your old job back." He paused, letting his lies sink in. When she didn't spit in his face, he added, "It would be like none of this ever happened. You and I would be a team again. What do you say?"

"Are you insane?"

He whirled on her, his face suffused with anger. "Am *I* crazy? Let's rewind for a second. Who thought who was here to kill them?"

"In my defense," she said, "someone took a shot at me this afternoon. I assume that someone was you. Was I wrong?"

"Wait … what?" His anger vanished. "Someone shot at you?" The concern in his eyes caused Six to punch him in the arm. Ben ignored the puny hit and, moving several flimsy garments aside, settled into the desk chair. "Tell me what happened."

With a sigh, she launched into the story, not quite sure if she believed his innocent act. Her getting shot at on the day he showed up in paradise seemed like too much of a coincidence for her peace of mind. Ben knew how to lie without breaking a sweat. She'd watched him do it a million times. But what if he was telling the truth? What of Ben really did want her to go back to D.C.? A lump formed in her throat. Part of her wanted nothing more than to turn back time, to follow him home like an eager puppy. Hell, in a few more minutes, she'd be on her back begging for a belly rub. The thought brought a rush of heat to her cheeks.

Taking a deep breath, she told him about the near-fatal attempt on the volcano earlier today. His face grew cold when she reached the part about her and Zach's ill-timed kiss.

When she finished, he asked a few questions, his voice coldly professional. "What caliber weapon?"

"Small. Maybe a .22." She shrugged. "A few inches left and we wouldn't be having this conversation."

He leapt to his feet in one sleek motion with the fleetness of a cat, one less well-fed than her fat tabby cat. "I need to make a call. Stay put," he ordered, his tone brooking no argument.

Rather than resist the inevitable, she nodded. Ben gave her a slow smile and left the room.

When Ten saw Ben, the younger man jumped to attention. "Sir?" he said.

"Watch her," Ben said, motioning to the open doorway. "If she tries to leave, stop her." In case Ten decided 'stopping' her meant shooting her dead, the older assassin removed the clip from his partner's weapon and emptied the shells before returning it to the holster at his side, all of which Ten failed to notice.

The kid's attention was totally focused on the interior of the hotel room, where Six stood next to the bed, stripping out of her sundress and pulling on a tank top and shorts.

Ben swallowed, hard, but managed to tear his eyes away from the sight of a half-naked Six and the infinity symbol tattooed on her lower back where her spine met the luscious curve of her butt. *That's new*, he thought, as his blood pressure spiked.

"Sir? I don't think ..." the kid muttered as if in pain.

Ben blew out a harsh breath, just as lust-filled as the kid. Or maybe he just hid his reaction better. At least he hoped he did. It wouldn't do for Six to learn of his physical attraction to her. Not now. Not when he needed the upper hand. He'd had a hard enough time hiding how attracted he was to her six months ago. Add to that her deliberate attempts at seduction, and Ben would end up drooling like a teenager, much like the kid standing next to him.

Poor Curtis just wasn't cut out for this work. He looked as if he might cry, so Ben did what any assassin worth his salt would do, he gave the kid a smack upside the head, mentally giving himself an even harder whack. "Just don't let her out of your sight. I'll be back as soon as I can."

Chapter 13

~~

T WENTY MINUTES LATER, SIX, dressed in a white tank top
and a pair of gym shorts, stepped into the hallway where
Curtis stood guard. The kid reached for his gun, but she waved
him off. "I'm going to order a snack from room service," she
said with a yawn. "Would you like anything?"

"No ma'am." His eyes stared at the floor.

She took a step closer, her hand caressing the hard muscles
of his shoulder. "Are you sure? Maybe a cold beer? It sure is hot
out." She used her other hand to fan the swell of her breasts
above her tank top. "I hate to think of a big guy like you sitting
out here all night, thirsty."

Beads of sweat popped out on Curtis' forehead. He seemed
to consider her offer, his eyes darting back and forth like those
of a child debating good versus evil and, in the end, choosing
the dark side. "One drink couldn't hurt," he said, following her
into the hotel room. The door closed quietly behind them.

$\oplus$

"DON'T LIE TO ME, Parker. You sent someone after her," Ben

yelled into the secure phone line. "I said I would handle it." Damn it, he needed her alive, at least for now.

The crackle of static buzzed through the line as did Parker Langdon's sleepy voice. He neither validated nor denied Ben's claim. "Have you located Ms. Winslow?"

"No."

For a few seconds absolute silence met his statement. Finally Parker sighed. "Is Agent Winslow worth your career? We need this mess cleaned up. Whatever it takes. Now. Today. Lives are at stake." After a pause, he added in a voice vibrating menace, "She's already almost cost you your life. Next time she just might succeed. Remember that, Agent Miller."

As if Ben could forget.

⊕

"THAT HITS THE SPOT," Curtis said, gulping down the rest of a glass of ice-cold coconut milk. He sat in a high-backed chair in Six's hotel room, his massively muscled legs resting on a leather ottoman. She sat on the bed opposite him, her slender legs crossed daintily at her ankles.

How Curtis wanted to touch those long, tanned limbs. She was perhaps the most beautiful woman he'd ever seen, or at least the best looking to ever give him the time of day. Those lips begged to be kissed and those eyes were the color of the deepest of oceans. Her dark hair fell around her shoulders in waves. He stared at a delicate curl right above her breast, a curl that just begged to be stroked. The moonlight from the open window kissed her bronzed skin, causing a stirring in his groin.

"How long have you worked with Ben?" she asked, taking a sip from her own beverage, her first alcohol of the night, a frosty Fire Rock Pale Ale. The foam curled across her lips.

Curtis's head swam. He wanted her. Wanted her right now.

She repeated her question in a silken whisper.

"Oh," he scratched his shaved head, "about a month. They

assigned me to Miller right after training." He paused, running his tongue along his thin lips. "Can I ask you something?"

"Of course." She smiled, uncrossing her legs. "My life's an open book."

He swallowed, nearly choking on his own saliva. "What's with the numbers?"

She tilted her head. "What'd you mean?"

"Miller and the numbers." He rubbed his eyes, which had started to blur. He blinked to clear his vision. "He calls you Six, me, Ten. What's that about? Is he OCD or something?"

"Or something," she said with a bitter laugh. "Ben worked for OPS for two years before we met. In that time they'd partnered him with five other agents. Most of them …. Well, let's just say they didn't work out."

"What, like, he got sick of them?"

Six shook her head. "No, like, they died."

"Jesus." He crossed himself. "Was Miller responsible?"

"Of course not," she said, a hint of steel in her voice. "Ben Miller is the best assassin alive. His partners screwed up, and they died. Simple as that."

"Then what's with the numbers?"

She closed her eyes, a deep sadness weighing on her. "Numbers don't matter." To Ben she had always been a number between five and seven. Nothing more. Her heart squeezed at the thought. His casual arrival on the island proved as much. One way or another, Ben always got what he wanted, and right now he wanted her dead.

Ten shook his head, back, forth, and back again. "I don't follow."

"When you know someone's name, even if you hate them, they matter. They have power over you." She smiled sadly. "Numbers don't. They don't matter."

"That's cold." Curtis rose from his chair, swaying slightly. His head felt like lead, as did his stomach. What kind of degenerate was he working with? He didn't want to be another number. Especially not a dead number.

He stumbled toward her, but stayed on his feet. She would save him. That's why he was here. She would be his salvation, his way out of the mess he was in, if only he could touch her. "Please …" he whispered. Bumping the edge of the bed, he tipped forward, landing on top of her warm, beautiful body.

"Shhh. Relax," she whispered, stroking the back of his neck. "Let it work."

It? What it? Darkness blanketed his vision, and Curtis slowly spiraled into oblivion.

Chapter 14

~~~

Ben returned to Six's hotel two hours later. The hallway outside her room was empty. He closed his eyes and prayed, for patience as well as Ten's continued breathing. He doubted Six would kill the kid, not that she wasn't capable of the dastardly deed. Hell, he'd seen her snap the neck of a man twice her size in one fluid motion without breaking a single nail.

Present love-interest, Zach, aside, Six wasn't stupid. Killing Ten would bring on the wrath of OPS, not to mention Ben, faster than she could handle.

Besides, if anyone deserved the right to kill Ten, it was Ben. His bullet-riddled shoulder ached every morning since the accident, a daily reminder of what he'd lost when Six had turned traitor.

Here goes nothing, he thought as he slammed the heel of his boot against the lock of the hotel room door. It flew inward, smashing against the woodwork with a loud bang. He drew his gun, shielding his torso with the wall. In his heart, he knew Six was long gone, but he wasn't about to take the chance of a bullet between the eyes from the semi-scorned assassin. He was also far from stupid.

Slowly he entered the room, scanning it with his 9mm. Ten lay face-down on the bed, still breathing, if the gentle snores escaping his mouth were any indication. Ben shook his head and lowered his weapon. Crossing the room, he lifted a single sheet of paper from the dresser. It read, "Lorazepam 3mg."

Crumpling the paper in his hand, he grabbed the phone and dialed the front desk. "Room 403," he said when they answered. "I need a pot of coffee. Black. And directions to the nearest air strip." He paused, listening to the sweet yet tired woman on the other end. "No, not the airport. An airfield. The kind of place where you can rent a single engine plane."

Or steal one.

⊕

SIX BOUNCED ON THE seat of the hotel shuttle van as the driver, Emilio, apologized for every bump in the dirt roadway. "They don't maintain the road, miss," he said with an apologetic shrug. "Are you sure you wouldn't rather wait at the airport? They have a flight to the mainland that leaves at five a.m. That's only two hours from now."

Two hours too long.

Once Ben realized she was gone he'd be on her trail in no time. That left her with few options. The Pukui Air Field offered the perfect solution in the form of a Cirrus SR20. A SR20 flew for 2,000 miles on a single tank of fuel, enough to get her safely to the mainland.

Once she landed, she would change identities again and slip off the radar. Maybe head to Canada. After all, hockey season had just started, eh?

The van hit another rut, sending her tumbling to the floor. Her knee slammed into the ground, leaving a large welt.

Emilio hit the brakes and rushed to her aid. "Oh, miss, you're bleeding," he said, gesturing to the cut on her shin where a small droplet of blood rose from her pale skin.

"I'm all right," she assured him, wiping the blood off with the sleeve of her sweater. "Please. I don't have much time."

His eyes narrowed with concern and a hint of suspicion, Emilio returned to the driver's seat. As the van started back up the rocky road, the sound of crickets and ocean waves pounding along the jutting coastline drowned out every other noise except for the whine of the shuttle's engine.

Six replayed the last couple of hours in her head. She felt bad about drugging Curtis, but she needed to get away, if only from temptation. A part of her wanted nothing more than to trust Ben, to run back to the safety behind the barrel of a sniper rifle. Killing at 1,000 yards was easy, unlike life.

She thought of her new friends, about Zach and his sweet smile and gentle kisses. Would she miss them? Would they miss her? She wanted to believe so.

She smiled at the memory of running into Zach in the hotel lobby an hour ago as she made her grand escape. His slurred inappropriate suggestion had made her laugh, but she didn't have time to enjoy his antics. She had to disappear and quickly before Ben ended whatever game he was playing and finished her off.

The flash of headlights from behind the van brought her back to the present with a strong sense of dread. The interior of the shuttle van lit up with an intense glow.

"Stupid *ha'ole*," Emilio said. "Drive too fast on this road you end up dead."

The hairs on her arms rose. A kick of adrenaline hit her bloodstream. Her vision narrowed seconds before impact. The vehicle behind them smashed into the rear quarter panel of the shuttle van in a typical PIT maneuver. A ploy used by cops to stop high-speed chases without killing innocent motorists.

Metal screeched as the two vehicles veered off course. Emilio muttered a string of curses, fighting to regain control before the van slipped over the side of the mountain.

But it was too late. The van careened off the road, striking a tree and then spinning into a boulder the size of Gibraltar before it flipped over and made its descent down the mountain.

Six tumbled over and over again, crashing into the roof like a rag doll. She tried to protect her head, wrapping her arms around her skull. Her shoulder snapped under the assault, leaving her helpless as the metal of the van twisted beneath her.

Pain ripped through her side, which quickly turned sticky and wet with blood. And still the van continued downward, twisting and tearing its metal frame. The window next to her exploded, showering her with glass. Smoke and the rusty taste of blood filled her mouth. *This is it*, she thought as the van rotated 360 degrees in the air. Six closed her eyes and waited for death.

As if by some miracle, the van's spiral suddenly stopped as the vehicle came to rest at the bottom of a ravine. Smoke bellowed from its crumpled engine. The only sound was the wobble of the still spinning tires.

She wiped a smear of blood from her eyes, checking her body for injuries. Puncture wound below her ribcage. Superficial cuts and bruises.

She'd live.

She gazed up at the headlights on the rise above the van.

Maybe.

Chapter 15

~~

FRANTICALLY SIX SEARCHED FOR her weapon in the twisted wreckage. Finding none, she scooted forward, carefully picking her way to the driver and his two-way radio. Emilio lay unconscious or maybe dead in the driver's seat, his seatbelt securely fastened.

"Emilio," she groaned, "answer me, please." She bit back a scream of pain as shards of glass cut into her hands and knees. She had to keep moving. Had to get the driver to safety. Somewhere outside, an assassin lurked, ready and willing to kill anyone who got in his way. She wouldn't be responsible for another innocent man's death.

She inched a few more feet, close enough to see the glowing dial on the speedometer. The pain in her body was almost unbearable. Her stomach threatened to rebel, and bile rose into her throat.

Instead of puking, she picked option B.

She blacked out.

⊕

Upon regaining consciousness, Six reached for the gun she'd found lying in a pile of metal scraps. Sometime later, a flash of light swept over the crumpled vehicle. The fingers of her hand curled around the grip of the gun as she took shaky aim at the light.

Killing her wouldn't be easy.

Raising her weapon with a quivering arm she took aim at the broken windshield. A shadow passed by, obscuring the silvery moonlight. Her finger tightened on the trigger.

⊕

"Hold your fire," Ben yelled over the pop of gunfire from inside the crushed shuttle, which lay broken and battered on its side. Rather than the chilling fear he'd felt since arriving at the accident scene, he felt almost giddy. Six was alive and she'd tried to blow his head off.

A good sign.

He jumped on top of the passenger side of the van. It shifted under his weight, threatening to topple. He stood perfectly still until the vehicle settled, then slipped through the broken side window.

Glass littered the ground, sharp shards ready to tear into the tough leather of his boots. He noticed Six right off. She looked half-dead, blood covering her face, hands, and body, but she held her weapon steady, aimed at his heart. His relief faded some. "You all right?"

"I've been better." Her tone of voice all but accused him of crashing the van. "How'd you find us?" She motioned with the gun.

His face tightened. "Van's got GPS." He nodded at the blinking light on the dashboard in case she didn't believe him. "Medics are on the way. Just hang in there." Crawling carefully through the twisted metal, he knelt down next to her, ignoring the weapon, inches from his chest. He understood her need for control, for self-protection. In her situation—second murder attempt in two days—he doubted he'd lower his weapon either. He scanned her blood-soaked body for damage. "Can you walk?"

She nodded. "Emilio."

At his blank look, she motioned to the driver strapped in his seat. "Got him," he said, heading for the injured driver. He checked the man for a pulse, finding it strong and steady under his fingertips. A stream of blood ran down his forehead and into the collar of his shirt. "Emilio," he said, giving the man's cheek a light tap. "Can you hear me?"

Emilio groaned.

"That's good." Ben pulled the man's eyelid up, checking for pupil reaction. Thankfully Emilio responded by feebly pushing at Ben's hands. "He's good," he said to Six and was rewarded by her sigh of relief.

He moved back to Six. He winced at the sight of her in the heavy moonlight. Blood and tears streaked her face. In three years of knowing her, this was the first time he'd seen her in tears. A sight he never wanted to see again. Tears weren't his partner's style. She was cold and hard. A total control freak. Her sudden vulnerability jolted him from his normally detached demeanor.

He bit his lip. "Just relax. You'll be at the hospital soon enough." The blare of sirens rushing up the road confirmed his promise.

FOOTSTEPS RESOUNDED OVERHEAD. HE leapt to his feet, his gun at the ready, until he saw the flashing lights of a crowd of emergency vehicles. "Down here," he yelled, waving his arms.

He turned to smile at Six. She lay on the ground, eyes closed, face slack, as if dreaming innocent dreams.

Instead, she was reliving the nightmare that had become her life. A nightmare that would only get worse, he thought grimly.

⊕

THE SEEMINGLY ENDLESS NIGHT came to a close a few hours later as Ben helped Six out of a taxi and into the lobby of the resort. Pricked, poked, X-rayed, and cleaned up, she emerged from the hospital with a bruise the size of Texas on her forehead and a bottle of painkillers in her pocket. Emilio wasn't so lucky. The poor man would remain in the hospital overnight.

Ben had tried to insist that his ex-partner remain in the hospital as well, but she'd refused. Violently. In fact, his arm bore a fist-shaped bruise, proving just how much she disagreed with his opinion. The doctor at the hospital was of the same opinion until she threatened him with even greater bodily harm. Thirty minutes later the hospital released her with little fanfare.

Now in the lobby of the hotel, Ben helped her into the elevator and pressed the button for the fourth floor. He gave her a small, encouraging smile. Besides looking exhausted, she had faint lines of pain etched along her mouth and eyes. Yet, she still looked beautiful to him. A new feeling rose inside him. A new unwelcome feeling. Tenderness mixed with more than a little lust.

It scared the hell out of him.

What was wrong with him? Six was a pawn, a means to an end for him, an injured means, and very likely a traitor to her country. Not to mention that emotions held no place in the life of a killer. Then there was the fact that the object of his pity and his desire had a target the size of a serving platter on her back and knew ten ways to kill a man with her thumb.

He rubbed his eyes. Exhaustion was affecting his judgment, that was all. After a few hours' sleep he'd forget all about her endless legs or the way the right side of her mouth tilted a bit higher than the left when she grinned.

Six snapped her fingers in front of his face and then winced. "Earth to Ben."

"Sorry," he said, running a hand over his face. "Were you saying something?"

Her cherry lips, which he couldn't stop staring at, pulled into a frown. "Hey," she said, "I'm the one with the head injury. What's going on with you?"

"Nothing."

"So you plan to spend the day riding the elevator up and down?" She motioned to the open elevator doors. A couple who appeared to be on their honeymoon—if their constant groping was any indication—waited for Ben and Six to depart, concerned looks on their faces.

Embarrassed, he launched himself out of the doors, leaving Six in his wake. The doors started to close behind him. She waved goodbye. He lunged for the door and missed.

"Shit," he yelled, running for the stairs.

He couldn't lose her again.

Behind him, the elevator dinged, the doors sliding open with a whoosh. He stopped and slowly turned around. She stood in the hallway, a big smirk on her bruised face. "Forget something?"

Chapter 16

~~

INSIDE HER HOTEL ROOM, dressed in a fresh tank top and gym shorts, Six sighed with relief, relaxing into the warm blankets surrounding her. Her body ached in places that only had names in medical textbooks, but she was alive.

It was an odd feeling to know that someone wanted her dead. That somewhere out there a killer waited. A damn sloppy killer, which did not describe her former partner. Ben was many things, but sloppy on the job wasn't one of them. If he'd come to kill her, she'd be dead already. So what did he really want?

She had a feeling that learning his motives would hurt her more than a simple bullet wound.

At the moment Ben was playing the role of her protector, saving her from the sloppy assassin. For which she was grateful. Until her body recovered, she wouldn't be up to leaping tall buildings in a single bound. She'd have to rely on him to do the heavy lifting.

For now.

But she wouldn't trust him. Ever again.

Lying back against the fluffy hotel pillow, she thought about

Ben and his reappearance in her life. A part of her had missed him, missed their easygoing relationship, and their uncanny ability to foresee each other's every move.

The other half dreaded the inevitable. They were, after all, two assassins with opposing agendas. That could result in only two possible outcomes. At best, he was here to drag her back to D.C. She didn't want to think about the worst case scenario.

Blood would spill.

That day in Arizona, the image of Davis Karter's face still vivid, she'd vowed never to kill again. But she hadn't counted on anyone finding her. Ben had—and so had another of their colleagues. Ben wouldn't hesitate to kill her if Parker gave him the order. He always completed his mission, no matter the cost. He never questioned his actions or those of his superiors. OPS provided intel and cash, and Ben followed orders. Because that's what soldiers do, and Ben Miller was the perfect solider.

At times, especially times like this, she hated him for it.

Why couldn't he see that someone at OPS had set her up to murder an innocent man and then put a price on her head? He knew her. Knew her like no one else ever had.

They were partners.

Friends even.

Or so she'd made the mistake of believing until the day he betrayed her.

She now knew where she stood in his life.

She was a number. A mission. Nothing more.

As if her thoughts had conjured the devil himself, Ben pushed open her hotel room door, stepped inside, and dropped a duffle bag on the floor. He kicked off his combat boots and then his Levi's.

"Whoa," she said, half rising from the bed. A wave of dizziness struck, and she fell back on the pillow. "What do you think you're doing?"

Instead of answering he stripped off his Nirvana T-shirt, which left him standing at the foot of the bed in nothing but a pair of black boxer-brief shorts and a 9mm strapped to his arm.

Six debated the wisdom of open-mouthed staring but decided that it would send the wrong message. "Ben," she began, hating the huskiness in her voice.

"Relax. Your virtue," he winked, "is safe. Partly because I'm exhausted."

"And the other part?"

He threw back the thin cotton sheet covering her and shoved her 9mm under the pillow next to her. "I don't wanna hurt your feelings."

"Try me."

"You look like crap." He motioned to her bruised face. "And not just 'wake up in the morning after a one night stand' sort of crap either. But the 'hell has no fury' kind."

She clenched the blanket in her fist. "Thanks."

"No problem," he said with a laugh. "Now take a pain pill and go to sleep." He punctuated his order by sliding into bed next to her, dropping a pill into her hand, and flipping off the bedside lamp.

Exhaustion quickly overcame annoyance. She'd deal with Ben—his overbearing manner, his arrogance, and the very real chance that he'd kill her—later. But first she needed a long rest. She popped the pill and closed her eyes, while Ben's masculine scent surrounded her like a security blanket.

Slowly her fingers released the 9mm.

$$\oplus$$

AFTER A FEW HOURS of sleep, Ben woke, plagued with thoughts of what might've happened if the assassin had finished the job.

Picturing Six dead provided a much needed dose of reality. He vowed to keep her alive, while in the same breath promising to use her to destroy John Pillars. Needless to say, falling back to sleep would be impossible. Instead, as the sun set over the ocean, streaking the sky with vivid orange and pink ribbons of color, he put on a pot of coffee and headed for the shower to scrub his body clean of needless sentiment as well as dirt and sweat. Emerging from the shower, he yawned, secured the towel around his waist, and poured coffee into a cup. Droplets of water dripped from his shaggy hair, down his muscular chest, and disappeared into the terrycloth towel. He added a dab of milk to the coffee, two Vicodins and two Ambiens, stirring the mixture gently.

Somehow Six must have snuck past him, because she was apparently in the bathroom. He heard the water running in the bathtub. For a brief second he imagined Six, soapy and wet, her wavy hair brushing her breasts. He started to sweat again. Suddenly uncomfortable, he tugged at the towel around his waist.

Stop thinking about her like that. She's in trouble, he reminded his treacherous brain. Yet at the moment he wanted nothing more than to bring her to bed. His bed.

A knock sounded at the door, drawing him from his lusty thoughts. He reached for his weapon, flicked off the safety, and went to the door. Keeping his body clear of the door, he peered through the peephole and sighed.

Just what he needed.

"Yeah," he said, opening the door while keeping the gun hidden behind it. Everyone, even a jerk like the man in the hallway, was suspect. Though he doubted the tool knew how to load a weapon, let alone use it to kill someone.

Zach, dressed in an all-white suit with freshly pressed creases, despite the late hour, stood in the doorway holding a bottle of wine. His mouth dropped open when he saw Ben. "Umm ... is Linda here?" he asked, his hot eyes darting between the towel around Ben's waist and the unmade bed.

Ben conspicuously checked his watch. One a.m. He nodded toward the bathroom. "She's in the tub."

"Oh." Zach stared at Ben as if waiting for the punch line to a sick joke. The silence between them lengthened. Ben enjoyed every second of watching Mr. Perfect sweat. What did Six see in this idiot? He was no better than Davis Karter. Another shallow pretty boy with nothing of substance to offer her. Ben shook his head. Six had lousy taste in men.

Finally Ben relented when Zach continued to stand there, bottle of wine at the ready. "Can I give her a message?"

"Umm …." Zach took a step back. "Tell her we have a meeting in the morning. Ten a.m."

"Will do. Now you have a real nice night." He snatched the wine bottle from Zach's hand. "I know I will," he added, and then closed the door in Zach's face.

"Who was that?" Six asked from the bathroom doorway. She wore a white robe that matched Ben's towel. Her hair hung in loose, wet ringlets around her head.

"Room service," he lied. He dropped his weapon and the wine bottle on the bedside table and picked up the coffee cup. "Here." He passed her the cup, watching as she drank every drop of the drugged brew. Only then did he allow himself a small smile.

Chapter 17

~~

"YOU DRUGGED ME," SIX said the following morning. She'd barely surfaced from her sound slumber before making that declaration. Ben, the bastard, didn't even have the grace to look the slightest bit guilty.

Instead he shrugged. "Seemed like the thing to do at the time. Besides you're no worse for wear. In fact, you look a hundred times better than you did yesterday."

As much as she hated to admit it, she felt better too. Sleep, time, and pain pills worked miracles, she thought, until she glanced in the mirror. Then she screamed. "Oh my God. I look like I went ten rounds with Muhammad Ali. Why didn't you tell me?"

"I did." He walked up behind her and lightly fingered the bruise on her cheek. "Yesterday, if you remember. I specifically said—"

"Just shut up." She pulled away from his prying if not gentle fingers. "What did Zach say again?" she asked a second later as she pulled a light pink sundress over her tank top and shorts and removed the undergarments.

To complete her outfit, she slid her Kel-Tek P32 into the holster strapped around her thigh. The weight of the gun calmed her frayed nerves, but not enough to keep the agitation out of her voice as she repeated her question.

Ben was staring straight through her, as if lost in thought. She flicked her fingers in front of his face to snap him out of it. "Zach said there's a meeting this morning at ten," he said, adding, "Oh, he also said, and I'm paraphrasing here, 'I'm a douche.' "

"Really?" She tilted her head, a small smile hovering on her lips. "I'm surprised he'd admit it."

He shrugged again. "Yeah, well, unlike most of the douchebags you date he's a pretty self-aware tool."

"How New Age of him," she said with a grin. "But let's discuss something more important."

"Oh, but I find this topic fascinating." He covered an exaggerated yawn with his hand. "Unless you wanted to discuss hopping a plane and heading back to D.C.?"

And there it was. Game over. Ben wanted her to go back to D.C. Even though she'd known his mission all along, hearing him say the words bothered her more than she would have thought possible. Six stroked her chin as if mulling it over. "Since I enjoy Linda Burke's life," she lied, "I'd like to propose another option."

"Which is?"

"You walking out that door without looking back." Her eyes caught his, turning their banter from light to deadly in an instant. "Tell Parker you couldn't find me. Tell him you failed."

"Can't," he said, quietly, and with what sounded like genuine regret. She knew better. Ben wasn't one for recriminations or regrets. "Whether you want to believe it or not," he said, "you're in danger until we get to the bottom of what happened in Arizona."

"Danger from who, Ben? Am I supposed to believe you had nothing to do with the attempts on my life? That you're here to bring me home, and that's it?"

Ignoring her question, he paced in front of the window and then came to a stop, his eyes hard. "Come back with me." The unspoken 'or else' hung in the air between them.

Frustration stiffened her spine. "No." Each time he mentioned returning to OPS, she felt a rush of shame and fear. Soon she would have to face the consequences of running from OPS. But she hoped like hell today wasn't that day.

He blew out a long breath, his body relaxing. "It's a beautiful day. Skip your meeting with Zach and let's go have some fun."

She blinked at the sudden change in topic. "As lovely as that offer is, Linda Burke has work to do. All play and no work as they say."

"I'm starting to really dislike Linda." He frowned, lifting his gun from the nightstand and shoving it in the holster at the small of his back. "She's as boring as the halfwit she works for."

Six silently agreed.

⊕

"LINDA." ZACH WAVED TO her from across the nearly empty dining room. "Over here."

Six pasted a smile on her face, wincing as her skin pulled tight over her bruised face. She'd done her best to cover the large green and purple splotches with makeup, but judging from the horrified look on Helen's face, her efforts had fallen short. She tried to smile away Helen's concern. "I fell down some stairs. I'm fine. Really," she added before anyone could question her.

Zach shot her a frown but didn't comment on her ragged appearance or her late night hotel guest. "Now that Linda's here, we can begin," he said, pulling out a stack of paperwork. "Last quarter's figures ...."

She sat down next to Helen and ordered a cup of tea from a passing waiter. Her mind drifted in and out of the conversation around the table. Who cared about gross percentages and distribution points when, less than forty-eight hours ago, her new life had crashed in on her?

And it was all his fault.

Six glared across the room at her watchdog. Ben raised his coffee cup in salute. If only he'd disappear. Linda Burke was happy. Well, if not exactly happy, then content. She and her cat. She wondered if Sweetie missed her. Probably not. He wasn't the clingy kind, just like her. Two clawed peas in a pod.

I need a life, Six thought. Another new one. One without stalking ex-partners and killers, not to mention long-winded bosses fixated on last quarter's earnings. She suppressed a sigh as Zach went on and on about sales figures and market shares.

When he wound down an hour later, she excused herself and headed for the restroom. Ben was determined to dog her every step. The bathroom door closed behind her, shutting out his prying gaze. She sighed with relief until the door opened again. Helen walked in, her face lined with worry.

"Linda," she began. "I'm concerned—"

"I'm fine," Six said, looking in the mirror and reapplying powder to the makeup that did almost nothing to conceal her bruises. "I promise. I had too much to drink and took a tumble. That's all."

The older woman's eyes met hers in the reflective glass. "I took a fall a time or two too. You tell yourself 'be more careful,' but it's not your fault."

She frowned, unsure. "Helen, I appreciate—"

"Zach told me," Helen blurted, "about seeing you and your high school friend together last night. I understand. Sometimes you get swept up in the moment, and things happen …."

Six doubted Helen understood passion, especially the killing kind. She felt sorry for the dour-faced woman just the same. During the last six months Six had worked side-by-side with

Helen, learning all about her disastrous marriage and resentful teenaged sons. Under Linda's guidance, Helen had recently started dating.

She gave Helen a weak smile. "Ben would never hurt—"

"Shhh." Helen raised a finger to her lips. "You don't have to say a word." She patted Six's dislocated shoulder. Six flinched under the casual touch. "Just remember, you're a beautiful woman. You don't have to throw yourself at every man who looks your way."

"Umm…thanks," Six responded, confused. Did Helen actually believe Six would allow a man to abuse her? Apparently. She frowned. Not Six. Linda. Helen saw Linda as weak. A coward. Everything Six saw deep down inside Hannah Winslow, and hated. Right then, in the restroom of this five-star resort, Six decided to make a change.

In order to stay alive, she needed to kill.

One more time.

Linda Burke wouldn't survive the night.

Chapter 18

~~

Outrigger Reef Beach, Honolulu, HI
26Oct, 1600 hours

"DAMN IT, SIX," BEN yelled over the roar of the surf. "That's the stupidest thing you've ever said." The Hawaiian Koaʻe ʻUla bird flying overhead apparently agreed. It released a squawk and then dove into the ocean in search of its dinner. Ben went on, "I've seen you keep your head when other guys would've pissed themselves. Remember Kandahar?"

How could she forget? She'd killed six men that day. Six men who had lived and loved until she'd tensed her finger on the trigger, a coward hiding behind a sniper scope.

Closing her eyes, she swore softly. "You don't understand. You never will," she said. She opened her eyes to watch the bird as it dove again and again, always coming up empty. She knew the feeling. When the bird scooped up a small fish she resumed her run.

Ben was already a hundred feet ahead, too far away to have heard her comment. His tanned, broad back glistening in the sunlight was a sight to behold. Six caught up quickly, her aching muscles loosening with every footfall as she pushed through the pain of her aches and bruises. This was exactly what she needed. Pounding heart. Blood rushing with adrenaline. Breathe in. Exhale. Simple. Easy. No past. No uncertain future. Just this moment.

They ran up the beach, mile after mile, faster and faster as if they could escape the inevitable. The salty spray of the ocean mixed with the sweat coating their bodies.

Ten miles in, Ben slowed, a frown marring his rugged face.

"What?" she asked, jogging in place, lungs burning.

Rather than answer, he grabbed her good arm and pulled her against him. His mouth captured hers, rough, urgent, demanding, taking possession without remorse.

Surprised by his kiss, she paused for a second before responding in kind, her good arm sliding over his slick shoulders, pulling him closer. Closer still. Heat, unlike anything she'd experienced, coursed through her, clutching and tearing for release. She moaned low in her throat.

As abruptly as the kiss began, it ended. He shoved her away and swore. Six stood on the beach, her face pink with embarrassment and lust. Anger soon replaced both emotions.

How dare he? Without thinking, she attacked, the fist connected to her good shoulder smashing into his six-pack abs. "What was that?" she screeched, shaking her throbbing fist.

Doubled over, he groaned, his breath coming in short gasps, whether from her punch or lust she wasn't sure. When he recovered a few seconds later, he straightened, shooting her a sheepish look. "Sorry."

"Sorry?" She took a menacing step toward him. "Is that all you can say? You kissed me!"

"Yeah." He winced. "I did."

All the anger drained out of her body, leaving her confused and exhausted. "Why?"

For a minute he said nothing, keeping his gaze locked on

the ocean waves as if they held the words he either couldn't confess, couldn't express, or didn't understand. "You're not a coward," he said, his voice as harsh as the roaring surf.

"What?"

"You're not a coward," he repeated. "When you called yourself a coward earlier, I …. You're not weak."

She swallowed. How she wished what he said was true. But she knew better. Deep down. Confronting death was the easy part. The emotional stuff, like her guilt over Davis' death, terrified her.

For as long as she could remember, whenever anything got emotionally sticky, she would run like a frightened child. The disaster at OPS was a perfect example. Rather than answer the charges against her, she'd chosen to make a run for it, leaving unanswered questions and a killer in her wake.

Questions with answers that were better left unspoken.

Her eyes drifted to the man standing next to her in the warm sun.

Ben had given the order to shoot.

She took the shot.

Davis had died.

She closed her eyes, and for the first time, Hannah Winslow stopped running.

⊕

BEN TOOK A DRINK from an icy bottle of Fire Island Pale Ale, his eyes locked on the woman next to him. Kissing her on the beach earlier had been a tactical error. Six wasn't the kind of woman to let sex rule her. A pity, to be sure.

But damn it, he'd nearly lost it on the beach. She'd called herself a coward. He'd tried to forget her words. To run and run until his anger dissipated, but it wasn't to be. No matter how hard he pushed himself, her words continued to haunt him, as would the taste of her, a heady combination of honey and sex.

"Davis wasn't in that bunny suit by accident," she said, raising her own beer to her kiss-swollen lips.

"I know." He paused to stare out the windows at the beach, crowded with tourists. Somewhere John Pillars lurked, waiting for the chance to put a bullet in the woman next to him. Ben wouldn't let that happen. He'd kill him first. "When we get back to D.C., we'll find out why."

She studied his face, her eyes dark with suspicion.

Anger boiled within him. What the hell was this? Did she think he had something to do with setting her up to take the shot? He motioned to Ten, sitting a few barstools away, giving Six the stink eye. "Go for a walk," he said to the kid. "A long one."

Like a good soldier, Ten did as ordered. Ben waited until the kid disappeared before he pushed back from the bar to stare into her face. "Why didn't you tell me about you and Karter? Why did you keep your relationship a secret?"

Her face flushed red. "We ... I ...." she trailed off. Her eyes said it all. Whatever was between the two of them was off limits to Ben. "Davis is dead. My bullet killed him. Does it matter who knew what?"

He gave a bitter laugh. "It matters. More than you know."

She swallowed back six months of self-recrimination. She would not cry in front of Ben. Whatever she had or didn't have with Davis wasn't something to be weighed and analyzed by anyone, let alone him. "It won't change anything," she whispered.

Trying a new tactic, Ben grabbed her arm, which she quickly pulled away. "Don't you want to avenge him? To make things right?" He leaned in, his breath hot against her skin. "I can help you do it."

It was her turn to laugh. "At what price? My life?" She frowned, tilting her head to study the face of the assassin in front of her. "Do you think that whoever set me up to kill Davis is going to give up? That they'll let me walk back into OPS like nothing ever happened?"

Ben smiled. "I never said it would be easy. But nothing with you ever is."

"What's that supposed to mean?"

"After you left, I did some digging into the shooting," he said, quickly changing the subject.

Her eyes widened. "You did?"

"Don't act so surprised." He frowned, somewhat offended by her amazement. "I owed you that much."

"No." Six bound from her barstool, upending it. Ben caught it and her before they crashed to the floor. "You owed me much more. I trusted you."

He gave an internal wince but outwardly showed no emotion. Her anger was good. The madder she was at him, the less likely she'd be to let down her guard like she had on the beach. And he had to keep her on guard so she would stay alive. He swallowed an apology and said instead, "That was your mistake."

She gave a bitter laugh. "I won't make the same mistake twice."

For a minute, an eerie silence descended, as both assassins sorted through their thoughts. The quiet grew. As much as it killed him to do it, he was the one to break the silence. "This is the last time I'll ask, Six."

He didn't have to elaborate. His message was clear. Either she returned to D.C. with him willingly or else he'd force her to go back, dead or alive. Either way, he'd achieve his goal. She would pay for her sins.

"Do what you have to do."

He nodded, accepting her words.

She shoved her half-empty beer across the bar, and slowly stood. "I'm going to my room."

He set his own beer down, dropping a couple of dollars on the bar. The bartender, a young woman in her twenties with thick black hair, grinned appreciatively. Her dark eyes roamed over his Dirty Heads T-shirt and the muscular chest beneath it.

He grinned back, the way he might while appreciating a work of art—one he didn't plan to steal or sleep with. Turning back to his former partner, he said, "Let's go."

"Stay," she said with a glance at the bartender. "Finish your drink." Then, without waiting for a response, she walked out of the bar.

Chapter 19

SIX JAMMED HER FINGER into the elevator button and swore softly. She wanted to kick herself for acting like a jealous idiot, especially over a man who'd threatened to kill her moments earlier. What the hell was wrong with her? His threat hadn't fazed her, but one flirty exchange with a sexy bartender had nearly made her lose it. She blamed their earlier kiss. It had obviously affected her brain. Temporary insanity induced by raging hormones.

What was she thinking? Getting involved with Benjamin Miller was akin to suicide. The moment he'd touched her, she should've busted his nose, or at least paused before shoving her tongue into his mouth.

Her finger stabbed the elevator button again.

Emotions swirled within her. Anger. Insecurity. Fear. Sadness. Ben would have his way. He'd force her to return to Washington. Of that she had no doubt. By whatever foul means necessary.

Did that include kissing her senseless?

Of course it did. She gave a small laugh at her own stupidity. She'd seen him in action hundreds of times. He routinely rendered women helpless at his feet, all in the name of completing his mission. Again, she was nothing more than a number.

"Linda," Zach said from behind her. "I thought that was you."

Six turned around, praying the elevator would arrive soon. Pretending to be weak-willed Linda was the last thing she wanted to do right now. Not when she felt so raw. "Hi Zach," she said, eyeing his untucked shirt and the russet-colored lipstick stain on his collar. At least someone besides Ben and the bartender would get laid tonight, she thought with annoyance.

"I'm glad I ran into you," he said, grinning.

"Oh?"

He nodded, swaying slightly like a sailboat in the island wind. A sailboat with one too many umbrella drinks under its sails. "I wanted to talk to you." His voice lowered an octave. "About your friend, Miller."

"Ben?"

Zach flashed overly whitened teeth in a leering smile. "I did some checking. And I don't think you're going to like what I found."

The placating smile of Six's face froze and her heartbeat sped up. If Zach found out Ben's connection to the CIA, who knew what could happen. An outed assassin was a dead assassin.

"I think Miller is using you," he said.

"Oh?" she repeated like a parrot.

"Yeah." He took her hand, holding it much too tightly. "You know that I care about you." She frowned, not sure she liked where this conversation was headed. "I wouldn't want anything to happen to you," he paused, as if weighing his words, "or to our relationship."

Not in the mood to play Linda, Six hoped he would get to the point. The elevator arrived and a rush of people emerged, each dressed in the finest island wear—bikinis, flowered shirts, and enough suntan lotion to cause an oil slick.

When the elevator emptied, Zach waved her ahead. She entered, Zach right behind her. Out of the corner of her eye she noticed someone in the lobby, watching. Six gave Ten a small wave, thinking, *I really should apologize for drugging him.* She quickly changed her mind after the elevator doors closed on his one-fingered salute.

"As I was saying," Zach began once the doors closed, "I think we have a good thing here." He motioned between the two of them. "I don't want it to end."

Enough was enough. She placed her hands on her hips. "What exactly are you talking about?"

"Miller works for a firm in D.C.," he blurted out. "From what I've heard, he's a real killer. When he wants someone nothing stops him from acquiring his target."

A frown creased her forehead as her mind raced with excuses and explanations for Ben's 'career.' Had Zach really managed to blow their cover?

Zach was saying, "I think he wants you, Linda. And maybe the whole team. After what you did for H2, who could blame him?" He smiled, pressing the number four on the elevator console. "But I'm not willing to give in without a fight."

Whole team? She shook her head to clear it. "Fight?"

"I'll double Miller's offer, whatever it is." He grabbed her good arm, dragging her closer to him. He smelled of sex and whiskey, and not in a good way. "I need you, Linda. The team needs you."

Sick of being manhandled, she tried to pull away, but he held on tight. "Do you think Ben is trying to recruit me?" she asked. "That his interest in me is due to my skills at marketing bottled water?" Six's annoyance level rose while her self-esteem plummeted.

"Liquid refreshment," Zach reminded her, squeezing her arm much too tight. Her bruises ached under his fingertips. "H2 is a company specializing in 'liquid refreshment.' Any old company can bottle water. But our water is special. Purified.

From a Zen mountain spring."

Sales pitch 101. Her sales pitch, damn it!

"Listen Zach," she began, only to have her words stifled by his mouth, which smashed against hers in an inept attempt at drunken seduction. His tongue quickly followed, sloppily stabbing into her mouth. She considered kneecapping him, but before she could act the elevator doors opened.

A gasp echoed from the hallway.

She pushed away from Zach, her face heating up with anger. Standing outside the elevator, Helen also blushed as her hand flew to her mouth. She gasped, her arms fluttering with surprise. "Linda? How could you?"

Even though Six was two stops from her own floor, she leapt from the elevator, turning to face her boss and the embarrassed Helen. Zach looked stunned and terribly guilty as if expecting a sexual harassment lawyer to pop out from behind a potted palm tree. Helen, on the other hand, looked disappointed, as if Six had broken some sacred unspoken rule of womanhood.

Thou shall not screw thy boss in the elevator.

"Helen, I … we … weren't …" Six began, but Helen shook her head, punching the close-doors button on the elevator with a huff.

Exasperated, Six wiped away the trail of salvia left by her former boss and headed for the stairs, the plush carpet of the hallway silent under her sandaled feet.

Once inside the concrete stairwell, Six let out a loud sigh. This day was not working out as expected. First Ben kissed her stupid and then she followed suit by being stupid enough to want to kiss him again, even after he'd threatened her. Subsequently, Zach's sloppy kiss in the elevator and Helen's prudish response furthered her annoyance.

Could this day get weirder?

As if in response, the overhead lights winked out, leaving her standing in total darkness, the only sound, the click of boot heels on the concrete stairs below.

Chapter 20

~~

WHEN THE LIGHTS WENT out, Six dove to the ground, her heart hammering in her chest. What were the odds of a power failure just as she stepped into an empty stairwell? Slim to none. She'd long ago learned the dangers of coincidence. Like love, trust, friendship, or high heels, coincidence held little place in an assassin's life.

The boot steps grew louder, only a landing or two below her in the darkness. *Now or never*, she thought, leaping up the steps to the third floor landing. The flash of a gun muzzle filled the stairwell with a bright burst of light. A bullet smashed into the concrete a few inches from her chest. By the sound of it, loud and weighty, she guessed a 9mm. The assassin's handgun of choice. Seventeen shots.

Seventeen ways to die.

In the concrete bunker, the roar of the weapon was deafening, but it also gave her a slight advantage. Unless the shooter could see in the dark, he had to rely on the sound of her footfalls to pinpoint her location. The echo of gunfire had drowned out any sound, leaving her free to flee up the four steps between her and the freedom of the third floor hallway.

Surely the killer wouldn't follow her into the hotel. Taking a deep breath, she grabbed the handrail and rushed forward up the remaining stairs.

Unfortunately her plan had two drawbacks, the first of which she encountered when her fingers reached for the doorknob—the doorknob that should've been there but wasn't.

No way out.

Damn, the shooter appeared much better prepared to kill her this time. With a sick feeling in her stomach she wondered what else he might have in store. The answer came soon enough.

Another volley of shots rang out, smashing into the door next to her. She ran, ducking and weaving, to the relative safety of the next flight of stairs.

Pausing to listen, she strained to hear over the pounding of her heart and the ringing in her ears. She fingered her own weapon, almost useless in this situation. The killer was too far away and covered by darkness. Even if she did get off a shot, the muzzle flash from her gun would give away her location, making a bullet to her brain easier.

A moot point, she soon realized, when another shot pinged off the handrail in front of her. Darkness wasn't her friend. That much was clear. Either the killer had excellent night vision or, much more likely, a pair of night vision goggles.

The longer she stayed in the dark stairwell, the grimmer her prospects for survival. With each heartbeat the shooter loomed closer.

Do or die time.

She jumped up and ran, pushing her legs with every shred of strength, fear, and anger in her body. Gunfire ricocheted around her. Bits of concrete flew up.

Fourth floor.

A trip wire, invisible in the darkness, tore into her shin. The gash quickly filled with blood, running down her leg and onto the cold stone floor. She started to slip in the wet stickiness and stifled a scream. If she fell, she was as good as dead.

Luckily at the last second she caught her balance, and continued her desperate flight to the next landing. She had to think. The shooter wouldn't bar every exit. That would raise suspicion, right? She prayed she was correct as she lurched up the stairs like a drunken frat boy.

Adrenaline coursed through her bloodstream, banishing her fear and sharpening her focus. A plan formed in her brain. A risky one, but she had no options left.

Two steps from the next landing, she launched herself toward the door as she fired blindly into the darkness. The flare of her muzzle fire lit the stairwell with intense white light, blinding her but also her assailant.

Night vision goggles only worked in darkness. A flash of light was like a bomb blast for the retinas. Unfortunately night vision blindness didn't last, and the killer would soon regain his senses.

But she only needed a few seconds.

She reached the door, finding the handle—like the others— missing. Coldness crept into her. *I'm going to die*, she thought. *Right here. In a stairwell. In paradise.* Fate had an ironic sense of humor.

From two flights below the hollow sound of laughter bounced off the concrete walls. She shivered. A bullet whizzed past her head and she spun away from its searing heat. Her head smacked the concrete wall and she fell to the ground, dropping her weapon in the process. The sound of metal hitting concrete echoed around her as her gun plummeted into the darkness below.

Blood started to gush from the side on her head, streaming into her eyes and soaking her shirt. Maybe the bullet hadn't missed after all. Her stomach threatened to rebel, bile crawling up her esophagus like a volcano. Bells rang inside her head. They grew louder and louder, as did the footsteps of her killer, creeping closer. Hysterical laughter bubbled up inside her, but she held it back.

This was the end. She was going to die. Here. In a concrete stairwell. Anger briefly swamped her fear. *Damn John Pillars. Damn OPS.* She wouldn't go out like this.

The assassin's footsteps reached the landing below.

Chapter 21

～～

B EN STOOD IN THE hallway on the fourth floor, his arms crossed, waiting for Six. He glanced at his watch, noting the time, his heart pumping harder with each passing second. *Where the hell was she?* he wondered for the fifth time in the last minute.

When she'd left the hotel bar his mood had lifted. She'd reacted to his threat as expected, with stubborn determination, a trait he admired. She'd need that stubbornness to survive the next couple of days. For Ben was sure John Pillars would soon make his move to tie up the last loose end. Hannah Winslow. Ben would be ready.

Using Six as bait hadn't bothered him. After all, she was a traitor to her country. To him. Until he kissed her a few hours ago. Everything changed when her lips brushed his.

Standing in the hallway, Ben began to reevaluate his brilliant plan. Six was still the key to catching Pillars. That hadn't changed. Now the question was, how much did Six know? Had she played him earlier on the beach, kissed him senseless to distract him from his goal? Was seducing him part of her plan? Or was the kiss real? Did it matter either way? Ben had his orders. His mission was clear. He would follow through.

He hoped like hell Six would make it out alive.

Shit. He glanced at his watch, then again at the elevators. Where the hell was she? He slammed his fist against the wall. He knew better than to trust anyone, let alone an assassin as smart as Six when she had a target on her back. Given half a chance, she would run, just like she had in D.C. And stupid Ben had given her a hell of a lot more than half a chance. He'd practically packed her suitcase.

Another thought crossed his mind. What if, instead of taking flight, she had done something even worse?

That something being Zachary Coleman Barber.

After Six had left the bar Ben watched as Barber pulled her into the elevator, his octopus arms wrapping around her body like he owned it. Ben had fought the urge to run across the hotel lobby and break Barber's pretty nose.

Then the elevator doors closed, and Ben slumped back in his seat, his mood plummeting. He'd left the bar immediately after Six, taking the second elevator to the fourth floor where he now stood.

He pictured her in Barber's arms and felt sick. What the hell did she see in those pretty-boys? Karter was bad enough, but at least the guy hadn't waxed his body from his eyebrows on down. Barber didn't deserve to breathe the same air as Six, and yet, every direction Ben turned, Zach was sniffing around.

Another minute passed.

Ben paced the hall, his mind filled with images of Six and Barber playing naked Twister in Zach's hotel room. Through his haze of anger a small pop grabbed his attention. Muzzled gunfire. He spun toward the noise, his adrenaline spiking, changing from jealous fool to cold calculating assassin in a heartbeat.

Pulling his 9mm, he flicked off the safety and chambered a round in one fluid motion. Cautiously but quickly he made his way to the fire door protecting the stairwell. The faint echo of footsteps and laughter reached his ears. A shiver ran up his spine. The wrongness, the kind that had kept him alive more times than he could count, washed over him like a wave.

He reached for the doorknob that wasn't there. Surprise registered in his brain. No knob meant a planned assault. A tactical hit. A true assassin, not like the half-assed joker they'd been playing with.

Had John Pillars finally made an appearance?

If so, Six was in trouble. She might even be lying there dead while he'd stood stupidly in the hallway. Ben kicked the fire door below the lock. The door caved inward, filling the black stairwell with white light. He quickly took in the scene playing out before him—Six, on her knees a few steps above him; a figure in black, two flights below.

Ben fired his weapon at the same time as the other man. A bullet whizzed by Ben's head, embedding itself in the concrete wall a mere inch to the right. Ben's shot also went wide, missing its target, but giving him enough time to grab Six's good arm and drag her to her feet.

Using his body as a shield, he rapid-fired into the darkness while pushing Six through the fire door and into the relative safety of the hallway. The pair of assassins landed on their backs on the plush carpet, both trying to catch their breath.

Ben's gun stayed trained on the fire door.

"I think we're clear," she said, her voice strained from gun-smoke and fear. He nodded but kept his gaze on the doorway. *Come on, you bastard*, he silently begged, willing the assassin to take a chance so he could blow him to pieces. And be done with it.

Ten minutes passed.

When it became apparent that the gunman wasn't stupid enough to barrel through the fire door to finish the job, Ben slowly rose to his feet. "C'mon sweetheart." He offered her his hand.

She took it reluctantly, as if he were diseased, and managed to stumble to her feet. Anger burned in his gut, an after-effect of the firefight. It took just one look at Six's bloody face before killing rage replaced anger.

Carefully he brushed a lock of hair from her cheek. Some bastard had tried to kill her. For real this time. No sloppy, half-assed job, but a full-on by-the-book assault. The kind taught by operatives during training by the CIA. Assassins like him. Had Parker sent another assassin? Or was John Pillars more than just a run-of-the-mill gunrunner?

The answer didn't matter. When Ben found the shooter he would destroy him with his bare hands, CIA or not.

Keeping Six close to his side and the gun in his hand, Ben pushed through the frantic crowd of tourists milling about the hallway. Half of the hotel must've heard his un-silenced weapon and called the cops. That was all they needed now—island cops with a lot of questions and an assassin on the loose.

The blare of sirens swelled in the distance as they reached Six's hotel room. The door swung open before Ben could unlock it with his keycard. Ten stood in the doorway, his weapon sweeping the hallway, his face as pale and clammy as Six's.

"I thought I heard gunshots. What happened?" Ten asked, his gaze locked on her bloody face. "Is she ... shot?"

The kid's face lost even more of its color, and for a second, Ben wondered if he'd pass out. Ten was definitely not cut out for the rough stuff.

"Ambush. In the stairwell. Cops are on their way up." Ben nodded to the elevator. "Go to your room. Hide our weapons and IDs under the bed between the mattress and the frame. Then stay inside."

"But—"

"Go. Now. If anyone asks, you know nothing."

Reluctantly, Ten followed Ben's orders, glancing over his shoulder as if expected the killer to appear out of thin air behind him. Ben waited until the kid's hotel door closed before he helped Six inside her own room. "Everything's okay," he said, not sure if he was talking to her or himself.

A half-smile flickered across her lips. "Easy for you to say." She rubbed her head, her hand coming away black with dried blood and a clump of gunpowder-singed hair. A perfectly straight line, as if cut by a razor instead of a bullet, ran from her temple to midway across her forehead. "Some asshole didn't just give you a half a mullet."

He couldn't help but laugh. "I'll admit it's not your best look." From the bathroom, he grabbed a wet towel and a pair of nail clippers, which he used to snip away the charred ends of her hair.

She sat up, wincing with each snip of the clippers. Thankfully the police sirens turned off, leaving the two assassins in silence. Six was the first to speak, sounding as if she sucked on a lemon as she said, "Thank you."

"For the new hairdo?"

"That too," she whispered. "I thought … for a minute there …."

He brushed away a lock of bloody hair from her face. "You're all right."

"Barely." She wiped her face with the towel, turning it rusty brown with dried blood. "This wasn't like the others. This guy planned for me to be in the stairwell. He knew my every move." Her tone was almost accusatory.

"Doesn't matter." And it didn't. Not to Ben. The shooter had sealed his fate the moment he targeted Six.

There would be no mercy.

She struggled to rise, her fear amplified by the coldness in his gaze. Whatever he was thinking did not bode well for anyone.

He reached for her chin, raising her face to his. "Six, I—"

"Don't." She jerked away as tears welled behind her eyelids, hating her sudden vulnerability in front of this man of steel. Ben didn't have feelings. He never questioned his actions or his desires. Whatever he wanted, he made happen at the precise moment that suited him. Anything was justified, as long as he met his goal.

This time *she* was his mission.

And she'd be damned if he'd walk away clean.

Chapter 22

~~

Ten's eyes darted between the bathroom door where Six was bathing and the window where the man he considered his mentor stood, gazing absently into the skyline. Benjamin Miller was one hell of an assassin. Smart. Ruthless. Fearless. Deadly.

Or used to be.

Now Ten, aka Curtis, wasn't sure what to think. Ben was protecting Hannah Winslow, a traitor by all accounts. Ten said as much once Miller hung up the phone with room service. "She killed a man. An agent," he said loudly, and then lowered his voice when the water turned off. "In cold blood."

Ben's face hardened. "Who told you that?"

"It's all over OPS." Curtis stepped back, unable to meet Ben's frosty eyes. "They say someone paid her to fuck the guy, and then when she got what she needed from him, she killed him for fun …" he trailed off.

"Not a bad way to go." Ben's lips formed a twisted smile that quickly became a frightening grimace. "But *they*, whoever 'they' are, got it wrong. Six is not that kind of girl."

"She drugged me and left me for dead!"

"She spiked your drink and showed you some leg until you blacked out," Ben countered. "Not the act of a murderous psychopath."

"Who's a murderous psycho?" Six asked from the bathroom doorway, her much shorter nail-clippered hair curling around her face.

Curtis blushed, his eyes riveted on the long legs beneath the white towel wrapped around her body. The swell of her breasts peeked over the top as if tempting him like Eve tempted Adam. Breasts. Apples. Really the same thing when one thought about it.

Curtis thought a lot about boobs, and sin.

"You." Ben laughed. "Ten was just filling me in on your nefarious deeds."

"Really?" She stepped closer, the fresh scent of ocean waves and tropical flowers floating around her. Curtis swallowed hard, trying to tear his eyes away but failing. "And," she tilted her head his way, "what am I doing in these fantasies?"

"Murdering a fellow agent," Ten said, avoiding her eyes.

"I see," she said, looking at Ten but directing her question at Ben. "Do you believe that?"

"Uh-I—" Ten stuttered.

"Leave Ten alone," Ben warned. "He's just an OPS puppet."

"Like you?" she asked, stepping closer to Ben, her movement exposing tanned thighs. Ben tried to glance away, but the sight of her golden skin held him in thrall, so much that he almost missed the edge in her voice. "What do you believe?" Her voice grew dangerously soft. "Am I a traitor?"

Ben swallowed. He wanted to deny it, to lie and tell her what she needed to hear, that he trusted and believed in her, but the lie stuck in his throat. Instead, he turned his back on her, directing his gaze once again on the bright blue sky outside the window. "I've seen the evidence."

Silence fraught with tension crackled in the air between them. Ten glanced at Six, noting the tight lines around her mouth. She seemed to be suppressing the urge to shout. But the expression on her face was nothing compared to the darkness in Miller's eyes. Ten went on high alert, preparing for the very real possibility of gunplay, his hand slowly finding the weapon at his side.

"Stand down," Ben ordered the kid, slowly turning from the sunny beachfront view to the deadly woman standing in nothing but a towel. Ben addressed her as if they were discussing the weather rather than cold-blooded murder. "I've seen the pictures, Six. The ones of you and Davis."

Slowly, as if the very act caused her pain, she nodded, remembering an afternoon picnic in the park, the sun shining, Davis' lips tentatively brushing hers. "We went out. Had a good time. I never denied that." Her fingers brushed the cotton fibers shielding her body from Ben's intense gaze.

"And the money?" He moved across the room, his hands fisted at his side. "What about the hundred thousand in your account? Money transferred from a bank on Grand Cayman the day Karter was shot?"

Her face paled. "I …. Someone must've planted it."

But Ben was far from finished. It was time to get it all out in the open. Every lie. Every half-truth. He needed to know what was real before he jeopardized the mission. "What about the files? How do you explain those?"

She frowned. "Files? What files?"

"The files on OPS." Anger and betrayal burned in his voice. "The files we found in your computer, detailing every weakness at OPS. A file outlining the cold-bloodied murder of an agent. A file with my name on it." He paced even farther away, as if he was afraid of what he might do if he got too close to her. "*Those* files, sweetheart," he said, the endearment sounding like a threat.

Chapter 23

✺

SIX'S FACE WAS BLEACHED of color as she sat heavily down on the bed next to Ten. "No. That can't be true," she said, softly at first, her pitch rising with each syllable.

"Ten," Ben said over her words. "Take off."

Curtis looked from Six to his superior, unsure. "But, sir—"

"Go."

Ten quickly rose to his feet, taking one last look at Six before heading out the door. When it closed behind him, Ben slowly sat down on the bed next to Six. He reached out his hand, but dropped it before touching her soft, golden skin. His desire for her was making him stupid. Trusting her, even the slightest bit, could get him killed, and yet, here he sat, wanting to do just that.

Six turned to face him, her eyes glistening. "Someone must've planted the files, like they did the money." She gripped his arm, her nails digging into his flesh. "I would never do that to … OPS."

He peeled her hand away, wanting to believe her, but not trusting himself, let alone the killer next to him. Even if she did look amazing in a towel. Droplets of water fell between her breasts with her every breath. He cleared his throat, trying to ease the tight feeling in his lower body. "Did you talk to Karter or anyone else about me, about us, or OPS?"

She shook her head briskly, sending her wet curls bouncing around her face. "It wasn't like that. Davis and I …we didn't talk about the job." Her eyes bore into his, willing him to believe her. "We went to dinner and the movies. Picnics in the park. Nothing more."

"I'll bet."

A dull red color spread over her cheeks. "We weren't sleeping together if that's what you're implying."

He gave a bitter laugh, hating the jealousy he suddenly felt for a dead man. He was losing his mind. No doubt about it. He placed the blame on the woman seated next to him for his sudden insanity. "So Karter was such a gentleman that he simply walked you to your door and gave you a chaste kiss goodnight?" His eyes slowly flickered over her towel-draped body, scorching her with his hot gaze. "No man is made of Teflon, sweetheart. Not where you're concerned."

Swallowing hard, she slowly rose from the bed, wanting to escape the heat in his gaze. She walked over to the window. Her fingers brushed the cold pane, willing away the achy heat radiating from her. An achy heat she'd never experienced with Davis. She'd liked him, respected him, but he'd never turned her on with one hot glance. Not like Ben. How could she make him understand without sounding pathetic?

She cleared her throat. "Davis and I …we just didn't …. One of us was always on call, or leaving the next day." She paused, running her fingers over her lips as she remembered their last date. "I'd thought … maybe that last night. All the signals were there, but …."

"But what?" he asked, his tone harsh.

She slowly turned to face him. "He left. He walked me home, gave me a kiss goodnight, and left. At first I thought he was distracted by his latest mission, but after he left, I started to wonder if, well, he just wasn't interested."

Not interested? Ben wanted to laugh at her obvious lie. He had a hard time believing Karter could just walk away. Hell, Six had likely betrayed him and her country, and yet, he still wanted to see her naked. He doubted he could kiss her and walk away, not without balls the color of a Smurf. He needed Six's help to draw John Pillars into the open, so he merely nodded as if he believed every word falling from her plump, lying lips.

Her eyes lowered to the ground. "I should've invited him in. Maybe he'd be alive if I had."

⊕

FIVE THOUSAND MILES AWAY, in an office high-rise overlooking the Capitol, Parker Langdon swirled his fifty year-old scotch around a crystal goblet. The amber liquid sparkled through the letters, OPS, etched in the glass. "We can't afford another mistake," he said to the man standing in the darkened doorway.

Paul Fuller stepped from the shadows, his expression as chilly as the night air. "Agent Karter's death wasn't a mistake, Parker. We knew the risk involved in his investigation."

Parker nodded, again swirling the dark liquor as if it held the answers to all his problems, or at the very least, the answer to his most current problem, Hannah Winslow.

He glanced at the red light blinking on his phone. Make that two problems. He picked up the phone, stabbing his finger against the red light. "Report," he said to the caller.

The phone crackled for a few seconds before the caller spoke. "We've located the target."

"And Agent Miller?"

"Yes, sir. Miller is on the island."

Parker frowned. "Proceed with the mission."

"But, sir—"

Rather than let the caller finish his statement Parker cut him off with a bark. "Report back once you've finished the job." He hung up before the agent could question him further, and once again faced his second in command. "It has to be done." When Paul failed to respond, Parker added, "You've seen the evidence, Paul. We have no choice."

Ben's mentor and friend nodded, gazing upon the heavy, dark clouds blanketing the city. "May God have mercy on their souls."

Chapter 24

~~

Halekulani Resort, Honolulu, HI
26 Oct, 2100 hours

MERCY WAS THE LAST thing on Six's mind as she and Ben argued later that night. "Damn you," she said for the tenth time in the last hour. "I won't sit around here, babysitting," she paused to give Ten a look of apology, "while you risk your life to track down *my* would-be assassin."

Ben laughed, both at Ten's glare and Six's words. "He's not *your* assassin. And, if I have my way, he won't ever be. So buck up and finish your game of Go-Fish." He motioned to the cards lying face down on the nightstand.

"Damn you!" She threw the cards in her hand at him. "I'm not kidding about this. The best way to trap this bastard is to use me as bait like we did in Rome. We both know it. Why can't you admit it?"

Ten ignored their argument in favor of the game. "Do you have any fours?"

"Fuck!" she screamed, jumping from the bed, and poking Ben in the chest. "Please. I can't take it. A bullet in the head beats winning at Go-Fish any day."

Ben picked up one of her cards and handed it to Ten. The kid nodded, sticking the four into his hand with grave concentration. "How about twos? She got any of them?"

"Ah!" She ran into the bathroom and slammed the door, hard enough to make flat screen TV on the opposite wall shake.

Ten glanced at the door and then back at his hand. "Guess not. I'll go fish."

Ben held his smile. "Take off for a little, while I deal with Mata Hari in there. Go grab a late dinner."

Ten dropped his cards and nodded. "Be careful, sir," he said, rising from the chair and heading for the door. "Women like her …well, they don't like it much when you tell 'em what to do."

From the mouths of assassin babes …. "Thanks for the advice," Ben said. "But I think I can handle her."

About an hour later, Ben realized how wrong he was, but by then, it was much too late for both of them.

$\oplus$

BEN THREADED HIS FINGERS through Six's short curls. "I like your hair." She'd done what she could with the nail clippers, but the end result had looked like something from *The Walking Dead*, so she made an emergency call to the hotel stylist. Now her hair fell in curls around her face, streaks of blonde strategically covering the worst of the missing clumps. The bruises had mostly faded, although the groove cut by the bullet across her forehead near her hairline was still vivid. At least it was a fairly clean cut and would probably heal without a scar.

"Thanks," she answered with a grin. "You're not so bad yourself." And he wasn't, dressed in a black blazer and Levis, his hair falling rakishly over one eye while his other eye sparkled with humor.

The sweet night air closed in around them as they walked

down the beach. Moonlight lit their path. Sure, it was a dangerous move, leaving the safety of the hotel while a killer lurked about, but Six couldn't stand wasting her last days in paradise, and maybe life, sitting in a hotel room playing Go-Fish with a kid barely out of his assassin diapers.

Soon she would return to D.C., willingly or not, to lose her freedom and possibly her life. But tonight, tonight she would enjoy the ocean breeze against her skin. Enjoy the warmth of Ben's fingers against hers. And, if she was lucky, she would enjoy watching her would-be assassin take a bullet to the head.

Because both she and Ben were armed with enough firepower to take down a small country, not to mention encased in two-inch thick body armor. Six hoped to lure the shooter into the open, using herself as bait and ultimately eliminating the threat.

Then she could figure out her next step.

As plans went, it wasn't the best.

It had taken thirty minutes of pleading and another ten of begging and threatening for Ben to agree to her plan, which basically consisted of them luring the killer in by saying, 'Here killer, killer,' or letting their actions say as much. Oh yes, and a promise from Ten to play lookout.

Ben wasn't thrilled with the idea or so he told her every two minutes as they walked from Six's hotel room, down the hallway to the elevator, and then out of the highly polished lobby. Or so he wanted her to believe. Since the kiss on the beach, Ben had been impossible to read. At times, she felt like his partner again. At others, like tonight, she wondered if everything he said was a lie, a means to further his mission.

"Watch your back," Ben said one last time as they stepped onto the moon-washed sand, his hand digging into the soft flesh of her bare arm. "If something happens—"

"This isn't my first time as bait, Ben." She patted his hand, causing him to flush. Her eyes narrowed, but she quickly shrugged off the twinge in her gut his reaction triggered.

"But if—"

"Remember Paris? That gunrunner at the nightclub? You weren't so worried about my safety that night."

His lips curved into a quick grin. "We never did find that guy's thumb."

"Well, he should've kept it to himself then."

He laughed, easing the tension between them. For a moment, he could almost imagine it was just another day, on just another job, with Six, his partner, at his side.

But it wasn't another day. Six wasn't his partner. Not anymore. She was a traitor. Nothing more than bait to trap John Pillars. Taking a deep breath he focused on the mission at hand, which meant keeping Six alive … for the moment.

⊕

To the rest of the world, they looked like a young couple in love as they strolled hand in hand across the moonlit beach. Helen said as much as she passed the couple on the cobblestone path. "Oh look at you!" she exclaimed. "You look so right together. Like you belong together."

Her comments struck Six as a little strange. After all, the last time she had seen the woman was after Zach had made a pass at her in the elevator.

The two assassins laughed nervously and moved deeper into the darkness, arm and arm, as one, one deadly team ready for a full-scale assault. More than ready. Six's body practically vibrated with adrenaline and focus. Having Ben at her side—his strength, speed, and skill—increased the budding excitement. She missed this. Missed him.

Too bad she could never trust him.

Not as long as OPS provided him with a steady income.

"Think he'll make his move?" she whispered, wrapping her hands around his neck. Ben responded by leaning down and brushing his lips against hers for all the world to see.

The kiss lasted seconds, and when he pulled away, she longed for more, though she'd take a bullet before she'd admit it. To Ben she was nothing more than a mission. A means to an end. A job well done. And she would be damned before being seduced and used by her ex-partner.

The very thought brought up a swell of emotions, the greatest one being full-on lust, as she remembered the feel of his sweaty hot and hard body against hers when he kissed her on the beach.

His eyes met hers in the darkness, snapping her out of her wayward, lusty thoughts. "Speaking of moves," he began, "I'm sorry about earlier. On the beach …."

As apologies went it wasn't bad, but it pissed her off all the same. She wasn't sorry about their kiss. In fact it was the best thing to happen to her in an otherwise crappy, terrifying day. She decided to ignore his attempted apology and focus on something more important. Unfortunately, her brain refused to focus on anything but the feel of his lips against hers.

Ben stepped back, pulling her arms from around his neck. "Stop looking at me like that."

"Like what?" Her eyes slid to his mouth.

"I mean it, Six." He swallowed hard. "This is a bad idea. Too much is at stake."

His words dowsed her lust as effectively as a cold shower. She instantly became aware of their barren surroundings. Anyone could be lurking in the underbrush, behind a palm tree, or one hundred yards away with a sniper scope. She shivered, wrapping her arms across her chest to ward off the night air.

Ben glanced to the left and then to the right then grabbed her around the waist, dragging her body against his. "Fuck it. You only live once, right?" His mouth crushed hers, hot and hard, urgent and demanding, as if he could kiss the past away.

Heat exploded inside her, burning like a wildfire, intense and consuming. His tongue swept her mouth, stroking and taunting, urgent with need. Moaning low in her throat she squeezed closer to the heat of his hard body.

She wanted him. Here. Now. The outside world disappeared under the burning between them. His fingers stroked her lower back, pressing her into his hard erection. She shifted her body to accommodate his hard length, her knees growing weaker with each caress.

When she felt as if she might burst into flames, he pulled away, staring into her flushed face, taking in her swollen lips and her fingers clutching the fabric of his shirt. "Six," he groaned from somewhere deep in his throat.

She blinked, trying to regain her senses through a haze of desire. "If you apologize again I'll shoot you in your sleep," she said, her voice husky with need.

Harsh laughter bubbled from his lips. "Wouldn't dream of it." His arms pulled her close again. His lips trailed a row of hot, wet kisses down the side of her neck. "I've spent the last few nights fantasizing about this," his mouth traveled to the swell of her breast just above the fabric of her dress, "and this." He squeezed her thigh.

She moaned as his hand moved to the swollen heat between her legs. Her thighs opened for him as if of their own accord. He smiled against her breast.

The sound of laughter twenty feet away broke the spell between them. "Shit," he said with regret.

Six stepped away quickly, righting her clothing, a flush of red burning her cheeks, her breathing harsh. Thankfully he seemed in worse shape, his breath came in short gasps as if he'd run a very long distance.

When she dared to look into his face, what she saw there both intrigued and frightened her. He looked ... desperate. She swallowed hard, releasing a pent-up breath. "We can't ...."

His eyes, glowing like emeralds, focused on her face, scorching her with their heat. Rather than argue, he reached for her hand. She paused, wanting nothing more than to accept all that he offered, to run upstairs and make love to him until they both burst into flames.

But something held her back. Fear. Genuine terror. For once in her life, Hannah Winslow was truly afraid. Afraid of what would happen if she said yes, but even more afraid of what would happen if she didn't. She wanted him, needed him like she'd never needed anyone. That realization terrified her all the more.

Staring into his eyes, she felt the fear that paralyzed her vanish, leaving her burning for the unknown. She took his hand, and together, the two assassins headed toward the bright lights of the resort and whatever lay beyond.

Chapter 25

~

Ben and Six made it as far as the elevator before he had his hands all over her, his mouth hot against hers. Wrapping her arms around his neck, she pulled him closer, enjoying the feel of his muscular body against hers. *Yes,* her mind whispered, and her body agreed, burning with desire for the man in her arms.

The kiss deepened as the elevator moved from floor to floor, occasionally stopping for new passengers, who took one look at the disheveled couple and politely pushed the close door button.

The elevator dinged for the fourth floor and Ben pulled away. Six missed his warmth, his fingers and mouth against her skin. He scanned the hallway, gave her the all clear sign, and then took her hand.

At the hotel room door, she stopped, her mind clearing from her lust induced haze for a brief second. This was a mistake. Ben had betrayed her six months ago. He didn't trust her and never had. He thought of her as nothing more than a number, and she had her doubts about his motives. Sex would only confuse an already deadly situation.

"Ben, I …."

Closing his eyes as if in pain, he said, "I know."

"So where does that leave us?" She hated the plea in her tone, as if all it would take was one little word and she'd get naked right there in the hallway. And she would have done just that. Her body burned at the thought of Ben naked and inside her, his strong hands stroking her to a fever pitch.

"I should say goodnight." He bit his lip, beads of sweat dotting his forehead. "Here. Before things get out of hand."

She nodded, unlocking her door with the key card then turning back to face him. "You probably should."

"I'm going to regret this," he said, watching her push the door open. His features grew rigid, his fists clenched at his sides. "For the rest of my life."

She laughed, low and deep, like a purr. "Probably."

He stared at her, his eyes glowing hot. A full minute passed, both assassins standing completely still. Ben broke the trance. "In that case." He pushed her into the hotel room, throwing her up against the wall with a gentle shove. His knee ran up the inside her thighs. The feel of his Levi's against her bare skin sent jolts through her already electrified body.

Before she could say a word, her sundress pooled at her feet, leaving her standing in nothing but a tactical Kevlar corset and black lace panties. Along with the shiny new Glock holstered on her thigh that Ben slipped her earlier. The alarm clock by the bed bathed her skin in a red glow.

"You're so beautiful." He swallowed hard before his hands swept over her flesh, stroking, taunting, and teasing. His mouth followed, capturing her lips as if he meant to devour her. Callused palms slipped across her heated skin, causing her flesh to pebble with excitement.

She moaned low and deep in her throat pulling at his jacket. "Off," she demanded, nearly ripping the fabric from his body. He smiled, that hot smile she loved, crooked and filled with devilish promise. Her own lips curved with desire as she tore off his blazer. His T-shirt and Kevlar soon followed.

Six ran her hands across his chest, loving the feel of his tight skin under her fingertips. Her hand edged lower to the thin trail of hair running from his belly button into his jeans.

His muscles constricted and he sucked in a harsh breath. "Do that and I won't last ten seconds. Then you'll be the one with the regrets." He trapped her hands, dragging them over her head, and buried his face in the swells of her breasts, his tongue hot and demanding against her.

Slowly, inch by tantalizing inch, he lowered her corset, finally taking her nipple into his mouth. His teeth caressed the sensitive flesh, branding her.

Her knees went weak.

Ben caught her before she hit the ground. "Bed," he said in a huff. She agreed, but her legs refused to comply. He seemed to enjoy her condition much more than was warranted. His husky laughter filled the room as he swept her into his arms and carried her to the bed, his mouth urgent against hers.

Wanting to prolong the moment and give them both a little oxygen, he left her, gasping, on the bed while he went to slide the French doors wide open and cool the heated atmosphere of the room. Then, panther-like, he stalked her.

At the foot of the bed, he stopped, his whole demeanor changing from lover to assassin in the blinking red light of the alarm clock next to the bed.

The alarm clock that read: *11:58*.

Chapter 26

~~

SECONDS LATER, SIX FLEW through the open French doors. She sailed over the railing and into the blackness below. A white light exploded in the night sky followed by an earth-shaking blast. Six felt herself free falling, hanging in the air for the briefest of moments before plunging into the unknown.

Her body smashed into what felt like a concrete wall, but turned out to be ten feet of chlorine-treated water in the resort pool. A wave swallowed her, forcing the breath from her lungs. She struggled for air; instead, her lungs filled with pool water. When her back hit the bottom she pushed off with her legs and rocketed to the surface, gulping in mouthfuls of night air.

What had happened? She shook her head, trying to comprehend the last few minutes of her life. Then a firestorm of flames and debris rained down from the sky like fiery shooting stars in the night.

That answered her question.

Bomb.

A flash bomb, by the smell of phosphorus in the atmosphere.

Someone had blown up her hotel room.

Tears and chemicals stung her eyes, blurring her vision as

her mind cleared and true terror set in. "Ben!" she screamed into the churning water. Her heart slammed in her chest, making each breath painful. "Ben!" she tried again.

Had Ben also landed in the relative safety of the pool? Was he, at this very second, unconscious and sinking into the bleach-filtered depths? Without thinking she dove below the blackened surface, searching for any sign of her former partner. Chunks of glass and charred concrete choked the pool, turning the water black.

She broke the surface again, sucked in a deep mouthful of air, and dove down for a second time. Searching. Scanning. Praying for any signs of life. Her mind, deprived of oxygen, swirled with frantic thoughts, pictures of Ben, face slack and blue, sinking deeper and deeper into the darkness.

Exhaustion stabbed through her body. With one last desperate attempt she dipped below the surface of the water, and there she stayed.

⊕

A MUSCULAR ARM GRABBED Six around the throat, yanking her from the water. She started fighting, biting, punching, clawing, anything to free herself and inflict as much damage as she could on the brute trying to choke the life out of her.

Once she realized the person attached to the arm was trying to help and not kill her, she calmed enough to glance up at her savior. A half-naked Benjamin Miller stood in chest deep water, his arm wrapped around her. A small smile curled his lips as he held up a bulletproof corset in his free hand. "I think you dropped this," he drawled, waving the corset around like a flag.

It took her exhausted, oxygen-deprived mind a second to catch up. She glanced at the corset and then down at her body, noting her bare breasts and soaking wet lace panties. Closing her eyes, she sank back into the safety of the blackened water.

"Death's too good for the likes of you," she whispered.

"I know." He reached for her arm and once again dragged her to the surface; shielding her body with his while he refastened the corset around her. "Apparently someone else disagrees."

Once she was dressed a little more decently, he searched her for injuries, *new* injuries that is. After all, she'd been shot at, forced off the road, shot, and now blown up, all in the last three days.

Six dreaded what tomorrow would bring almost as much as she dreaded leaving the safety of the pool. A crowd had started to gather at the edge, chattering about the explosion and subsequent fire, which the hotel sprinklers had extinguished in seconds.

"Planning to stay in the pool all night?" he asked when she made no move toward the ladder. "Not that I mind, but pruney isn't an attractive look on any woman, especially naked or nearly naked ones."

"Fine," she said, splashing him in the face with a handful of water before dog-paddling to the edge. She lifted her head high as she climbed the ladder. Leering looks greeted her half-naked exit. She bared her teeth at her new admirers in something approximating a smile. "Nice night for a swim," she said, grabbing a charred towel from a smoking beach chair and wrapping it around her body.

Ben followed her out of the pool, his grin replaced with a scowl of cold-blooded menace. The leering abruptly stopped.

Chapter 27

A FEW MINUTES LATER, Ben led Six into the hotel lobby, where confusion reigned. Cops and firefighters swarmed the building as desperate guests scurried from the smoky hallways. Ben grabbed a passing firefighter, doing his best over the constant screams of the fire alarm to explain their recent dive from the burning hotel room.

The fireman stared, disbelieving at first. But one look at Ben's charred Levi's, various scrapes, minor burns, and bruises, not to mention the gash across the back of Six's thigh from the plate glass window, must've changed his mind. The firefighter waved the paramedics over and left, shaking his head.

Ten ran into the lobby as the medics bandaged Six's leg. He jolted to a stop in front of Ben, skin pale, eyes wide. "Holy shit," he said. "What happened? Was it another assassination attempt?"

The medic quickly looked up. Ben shook his head and rolled his eyes as if Ten was crazy, which seemed to satisfy the medic. Probably easier to write up the report that way.

Ten repeated his question, and Ben rose from the gurney to frog-walk the younger man to an empty alcove by the stairs.

"Keep it down, kid," he whispered. "We don't want every cop in town looking at us."

"Sorry." Ten flushed, a dull red staining his cheeks. "But it was a bomb, right? Same as six months ago?"

Ben stared at Ten as if seeing him for the first time. Kid wasn't stupid, that was for sure. Rubbing his singed hair, Ben considered the recent bombing attempt.

Every bomb-maker had his own signature, the way he built the weapon or his choice of materials. In this case, the bomb in the Jeep and the one in the hotel room were both detonated with a simple electronic device. A cellphone and an alarm clock. Both easily accessible household items.

Much like the microwave bomb at Six's apartment in D.C.

Had she set him up? But why risk her own life? It was her hotel room after all. Unless she'd planned the whole seduction scene in order to rid herself of her former partner. He'd fallen for it easily enough, more than willing to make the same mistake Davis Karter had.

The mistake that had cost him his life.

The thought left Ben cold.

Chapter 28

〜

"Your name, miss?" A weary-looking cop asked, his pen poised above a frayed notebook. Six glanced around the lobby, searching for Ben, unsure what to tell the cops, even what name to give them. A cursory look at Linda Burke's identification would hold up, for a little while. Any deeper digging and the cops would expose her for what she was, a fake.

"Miss?" the cop repeated, his tone hardening. And who could blame him? A hotel room just exploded hours after a shootout in the stairwell of a five-star resort. Even the dumbest of cops might find a woman in lace panties and a bulletproof corset a bit suspicious.

Ben walked up just as the cop's hand hovered over the weapon holstered at his side. "Easy, pal," he said. "Ms. Burke's had a rough night. I'll be happy to answer any questions you might have."

The cop spun to face Ben, his fingers now mere centimeters from his gun. "And you are?" His tone implied Ben was an annoying tourist, one of those rich guys who used the island as their personal playground and let the local cops clean up their mess.

Ben grinned. "My name's Parker Langdon." He paused long enough to let the name sink in. "Special-Agent-in-Charge Parker Langdon. With the CIA," he added, in case the cop didn't get it.

"Yes, sir." The cop tipped his head. "Sorry, sir. Can you answer a couple of questions on behalf of your"—the cop motioned to Six—"friend?"

Ben nodded stiffly. "Ms. Burke is my secretary."

"Executive assistant," Six piped up.

Again Ben nodded. "My executive assistant. We are here on a working vacation." His voice lowered a few octaves. "You understand the delicacy of this situation, right? Taxpayers and all."

"Of course." The cop eyed Six's long legs under her charred hotel towel. "Taxpayers."

"Good man," Ben said, tipping an imaginary hat toward the cop. "I'd consider it a personal favor if you'd leave our names out of your report. Wouldn't want my wife to … misunderstand the situation."

Six held back a smile. Poor Parker … if his wife ever did find out. She almost felt sorry for her old boss, until she remembered he'd sent Ben after her, and then any and all of her sympathy dried up.

She flashed back to the explosion, to the feel of the glass door as it shattered against her body, to the smell of chlorine, singed wood, and burning chemicals weighing on her skin, to the choking fear that Ben hadn't survived.

If she didn't need therapy already, this past week would secure her a nice padded cell very soon. So many emotions ran through her exhausted brain. She wanted to curl up in a ball and sleep until the nightmare ended, until she woke up in her bed in D.C., safe and sound. Her body hurt. Her head hurt. Hell, even her toenails ached a bit.

But she couldn't sleep. Not yet.

She needed a plan.

$$\oplus$$

SATISFIED WITH BEN'S STORY, the police left a few hours later, and the hotel staff quickly escorted Six to a new room, on the second floor. Gone were the ocean views, but on the plus side, a fire extinguisher now sat on the smooth black desktop. Too tired to do more than smile, she let her burned towel drop and climbed into the large, soft bed. She relaxed against the pillows and closed her eyes.

A loud bang shook her from sleep and she sat up quickly, the sheet conforming to the curves of her body. Ben kicked open the hotel room door, his arms filled with bags of clothes, toiletries, and twin 9mm Berettas.

She was glad to see the guns.

"What do you think you're doing?" she asked, her voice shrill. She winced, trying to tone it down, but her next words came out just as tense. "You're not sleeping here."

Mostly because she needed time to recover from what had almost happened before the hotel room exploded, but also, to plot her escape. Never mind returning to D.C. She would never go back, not after OPS had tried to kill her. Again. The hotel room and the bunny bombs were textbook CIA. Same with the assassination attempt in the stairs. Parker didn't want her back in D.C., as Ben claimed. He wanted her dead.

What an idiot she had been. Ben shows up and suddenly all the reasons she ran from OPS in the first place vanish? She'd let him manipulate her, lie to her, make her believe in fairytales. The pain his lies inflicted surprised her.

Hell, for all she knew, he'd been the one behind the bombings. What better way to dispose of a supposed traitor? She shook her head. Her paranoia was starting to show. Ben wasn't the bombing type. No, he'd go for the quick, close-up kill.

But OPS had sent someone. Someone willing to kill innocent people to complete his mission. A man without a soul. Her mind flashed back to the hot Arizona desert and the rifle in her arms. Ben's voice crackled in her ear. "Take the shot," he said, and Davis Karter died.

Had Ben ordered her to take the shot, knowing it was Davis trapped inside the bunny suit? Was that why he was here now? To clean up the mess he'd created? She watched the assassin move farther into her room through fresh, wide-open eyes.

Ben ignored her, grinning at the fire extinguisher on the table. "What? No fruit basket?" he asked, dropping his bags on the floor and tossing the guns on the bed. They landed next to Six's thigh, bounced once, and settled, shiny and deadly, in the folds of the flowery design of the comforter.

She repeated her statement, her eyes never wavering from his face, "You can't sleep here."

Purposely misunderstanding her, he grabbed the pillow beneath her head and pulled. "Then I'll sack out on the floor." He tossed the pillow on the ground and kicked off his scorched Levi's. "Nighty-night."

"That's not what I meant and you know it." She scrambled from the bed, then remembered her near-naked condition and pulled the cotton sheet over her breasts. "I don't want you in my room. In my life."

"Hey," he began. "We've been through this—"

"I was fine until you showed up. Happy. And now this." She motioned to her charred hair and bruised face. Tears of frustration burned her eyelids, but she refused to let them fall. Instead she grabbed the TV remote and sent it flying at his head.

He ducked and the remote smashed into the wall behind him. "Happy? Really?" His bitter laughter filled the room. "What part of Linda Burke's existence made you happy? Even for a second."

She didn't mind the cat so much. Otherwise he was right,

not that she'd ever admit it. "I had a good job, friends." She paused, wanting to hurt him as much as his betrayal had hurt her. "A lover," she lied with a grim smile. "And then you ruined everything."

He froze, his face as hard as stone. "Lover? Are you telling me that you *love* that idiot Zach? That you're *lovers*," he finished through clenched teeth.

She nodded. Not that he cared who she slept with. She was a means to an end, a number, to him, but still she experienced a small degree of satisfaction when he flinched.

"What was last night then?" he asked, crudely. "Because you sure as hell weren't thinking of him when you had your hands down my Levi's."

She flushed from equal parts rage and embarrassment. "Don't worry about last night. It was a fluke. Won't *ever* happen again."

He shrugged. "Fine with me. You're not really my type. I prefer women who don't betray me. Or play games with my life."

She saw red. If a weapon had been nearby, she might have used it. Apparently Ben had the same thought, because he grabbed the Berettas from the bed and shoved them under his pillow on the floor.

Naked or not, Six rose from the bed, dragging the sheet with her. She poked him in the chest, hard. Stabbing her finger into the taunt muscles again, she said, "*I* betrayed *you*? Oh, that's fucking brilliant."

"What's that supposed to mean?"

"Doesn't matter." She shook her head, unwilling to let him drag her into that conversation. "You think this is a game?"

"Of course it is," he said in a strangled tone. "And I'm stupid enough to keep on playing. OPS could've sent anyone for you. But, no." He pushed her hand away. She half expected him to whimper like a kicked puppy. She didn't buy it for a minute. "I chose to come after you because I cared," he said. "A mistake I won't make again."

"Are you saying you *care* about me? Are you serious? Do you think I'll actually fall for that bullshit? The only thing you care about, have ever cared about, is the mission." She stomped across the room, pacing back and forth in front of the non-ocean view window. "I want you out of my life. For good. Forever."

Rather than argue, as she expected, he simply nodded. "Tell me where to find John Pillars and you'll never see me again."

She sucked in a breath, her heart shredding under the weight of his words. Ben believed the lies OPS fed him about her guilt. He believed she slept with Davis and then killed him in cold blood for a man, a ghost, she'd never met. A man Ben now wanted her to betray.

Until this moment, she'd convinced herself that he'd trusted her, even a little. But the truth was out. Everything he'd done—from saving her life to kissing her breathless—was done to complete the one mission he'd failed to complete, killing John Pillars.

"It's time to end this, Six." He took a step toward her, and stopped, his hands hanging loosely at his sides.

The tension in the room swelled, and in her exhaustion, Six wanted nothing more than to run into his treacherous arms and weep all over his hard chest. A temptation she resisted. Instead, she glared at him. "Way past time."

"Why are you protecting him?" He grabbed her arm, shaking her. "You're nothing more than a loose end to him. He's tried to kill you at least three times now. And he'll keep trying until you're dead. Protecting him won't help you."

"Believe whatever the fuck you want." She jerked away from his stinging grip. "But the only person I'm protecting is myself."

He stared unblinking into her eyes. "I will kill John Pillars."

And he would use her to do it.

The last bit of hope she'd harbored over the last six months disappeared under his steely gaze.

Chapter 29

〜

Halekulani Resort, Honolulu, HI
27Oct, 0900 hours

THE NEXT MORNING, SIX sat at a breakfast table, Zach and Helen by her side. Ben, across from her, was eating a large portion of eggs, bacon, and toast as if he didn't have a care in the world. But inside he was seething. *Damn Six.* She twisted everything around until he wasn't sure how to react.

Last night, she acted like she wanted him, almost as much as he burned for her. Then the hotel room exploded, and lust turned to distrust. They had almost been lovers and now they were enemies. He still wasn't sure how that happened. Not that it mattered. He'd vowed to kill John Pillars and he'd do just that. She would give him the information he needed to complete his mission. Even if he had to force it out of her.

For her own good.

As long as Pillars walked this earth, Six was in danger. And the longer she stayed in the cold, the more likely it would be that her death would be the end result. He didn't want her dead. The very thought turned his stomach. He slowly lowered his fork.

"The police said it was a meth laboratory that exploded," Helen said about last night's excitement. Her hand covered her mouth as if she held a deep, dark secret. "You know how those," she lowered her voice to a whisper, "people love to make drugs in hotels. I saw a whole *60 Minutes* episode on it."

Ben somehow managed to keep a straight face. *Those* people, the meth cooks Helen so carefully referred to, preferred motels that charged by the hour, not five-star resorts in paradise. But Ben was glad to know the cops had kept their promise, covering up the bombing under the guise of Homeland Security.

Zach shook his pretty blond head, making Ben want to strangle him with his bacon. "I'm just glad we didn't have to move resorts," he said. "For the amount of money I'm paying for this trip, I expect better than to be woken from a sound sleep and forced to evacuate in the middle of the night."

Helen nodded. "I had just taken an allergy pill, and then, *boom*, my window rattled. Scared me half to death."

Me too, Ben thought, *but for far different reasons*. When he first saw the alarm clock it took his blood-deprived brain a few seconds to process the danger. Then, when he did, his only thoughts were of Six. His body reacted instantly as he flung himself and Six over the patio, praying he'd correctly gauged the distance from the room to the pool. Thank God he'd opened the French doors, or they would have both been goners.

Four floors later, as water filled his lungs, again his only thoughts were of Six, an instinct that would be the death of him. And she accused him of not caring. In truth he cared too damn much. Why else would he have tracked her halfway around the world? Or risked his life to clean up her mess? Not that he'd admit as much to her. She had her lover boy Zach after all.

Ben sighed. Once Pillars was dead, OPS wouldn't care so

much about Six. He could convince Parker to let her be. To let her live.

"Linda, did the explosion wake you?" Helen patted Six's hand. "Being on the fourth floor, it must've sounded like a—"

"Bomb?" Ben suggested with a grin.

Helen smiled encouragingly and shoveled a forkful of scrambled eggs into her small mouth. Ben considered the bird-like woman. She wasn't ugly, just plain, especially seated next to Six, who vibrated with life even as her eyes shot daggers at him.

Ben hoped like hell OPS would let her live.

She glared at him, but addressed Helen's remark. "Ben and I were on the beach when the room exploded," she said, using the cover story they concocted last night. "We heard the blast and came running. We did have to dodge some flying glass." She rubbed the gash on her leg. "The fire was out in no time." With a sad smile she added, "The hotel staff refused to let us back into our room."

"For the best," Zach said, his eyes locked on Six's brand new bikini top, fresh from the resort's tourist shop. "I wouldn't want anything bad to happen to you."

"You mean, other than what's happened already?" she said, batting her eyelashes.

Rage twisted in Ben's gut but his face remained impassive. If Six wanted that nimrod, she could have him. Let Zach figure out a way to keep her safe. Because Ben knew—perhaps better than anyone—that time was running out. Langdon gave him one week to bring Six back. Failure was not an option.

Soon the island would be crawling with agents, even more so than now, all intent on one mission. As good as Ben was at his job, keeping OPS at bay while using Six as bait for Pillars would prove difficult, if not impossible.

Helen cleared her throat, and a flash of something crossed her face. But it quickly disappeared when Zach flagged down a passing waiter. "Mimosas all around. We're going to celebrate."

"Celebrate what?" Helen asked, clapping her hands together. An annoying habit, but one Ben found endearing. He wished Six would pick up a few more endearing, rather than annoying, habits. Since kicking him awake this morning, the nicest thing she'd said was 'Kiss my ass,' and that was only in the last hour.

Zach smiled at everyone except for Ben. "We're going to celebrate *us* and our long and happy future together."

"To our future." Helen raised her glass of orange juice.

Six smirked but raised her coffee mug. Her eyes met Ben's over the rim. *To having any kind of future*, she silently saluted.

Chapter 30

Six tried to pay attention to Helen, to the woman's inane, rambling story about her Chihuahua Peanut, but Six's mind began to wander as soon as Helen said the word 'walkie-poo.'

Ben appeared to be fighting the same battle against mind-numbing boredom and unbearable fatigue. His eyelids lowered to half-mast and his breathing became deep and even. If she didn't know him better she would've thought he'd fallen asleep. But he would never allow his guard down inside a crowded restaurant. Stab the guy at the next table, sure, but fall asleep? Never.

Shaking her head, she thought back to last night and his single-minded vow to kill John Pillars. More power to him. Hell, if she knew where Pillars was, or even what he looked like, she'd shoot the bastard herself.

Thinking the worst of her was bad enough, but his crack about her not being his type drove her absolutely crazy.

I prefer women who don't betray me.

Like he was some innocent dupe who'd never betrayed anyone, let alone sold her out to his precious OPS six months ago. What was worse, he'd done nothing but lie to her since arriving on the island.

And that made him so dangerous.

A few sweet lies and he could make her do anything before she knew what hit her. Her feelings for him, as confused as they were, could cost Six her life.

She needed to escape and soon.

"The water is crystal blue, like glass," Zach said, drawing her from her desperate thoughts. "The wreck is beautiful too. One hundred years of history just a few miles offshore."

She nodded as if she'd paid even the slightest attention to Zach's conversation. Helen, on the other hand, appeared to hang on every word; her eyes practically glowed with excitement.

"I booked us on the first boat out," Zach told Six.

"What?"

He smiled, patting her hand. "Weren't you listening? I asked you to join me on a scuba diving expedition tomorrow morning to this secluded little spot I recently discovered."

"Linda and I have plans—" Ben began.

"Yes," Six said at the same time, though the thought of spending anytime in the ocean, and worse, with Zach, made her want to stick a fork in her eye. Ben shot her a warning glare, which she ignored. "I'd love to."

A morning dive was the perfect cover for her getaway. She'd hire a boat to meet her a hundred yards from the wreck, sink below the surface and disappear for good. Divers vanished from the depths of the ocean all the time, even in paradise.

As soon as Zach realized she was missing, the coast guard would be called, and a search would begin, which would turn into a recovery mission after a day or two. Zach would be heartbroken for a minute or two, probably less, but he'd get over it.

By the time Ben realized her body would never be recovered she would be halfway to Brazil. Free from OPS. From attack.

From Benjamin Miller's heated gaze. This time he would never find her. She'd make sure of that, even if she had to destroy him to do it. Her chest burned at the mere thought.

"Well, it's settled then," Zach said with a smirk in Ben's direction. Ben glared back hotly enough that Helen let out a nervous laugh.

"I love scuba," Helen said, ever the peacemaker.

Zach smiled, shaking his head at her. "Sorry, luv. I need you here. For the conference call with Japan. We need those numbers and you're my go-to girl."

Helen's face fell, but she quickly covered her disappointment with a smile. Meanwhile the knuckles on the hand that gripped the stem of her orange juice glass turned white.

"Next time," Zach said. "Linda deserves a little fun right now. After all, this hasn't been much of a vacation for her. More like one mishap after another." Again Zach shot Ben a smirk, and Ben's fist clenched on the sharp edge of his own butter knife. A red welt rose along his palm and a deadly smile curved his lips.

Six shivered. If Zach didn't watch it, he'd find himself audited by the IRS right before a speeding ice cream truck ran him down. She'd seen it happen before.

Ben's ex-wife came to mind.

A year ago the poor dear had found herself under arrest for possession of illegal and dangerous animals after TSA agents found a stash of snakes in her Prada handbag. In Six's defense, the snakes weren't poisonous, just really, really pissed off.

"I understand," Helen was saying. "Linda's worked so hard to get where she is." Her eyes bounced from Six to Zach. Had any other woman made that statement, Six would've kicked her under the table, but Helen wasn't being mean. She didn't have a catty bone in her drab body.

"It's nice to know how loyal Zach is to his employees," Helen added for Ben's benefit. "He gives all he can."

"I bet he does," Ben drawled. "If you'll excuse me." He rose from his chair, calmly set the butter knife down on the table, and caught Six's eye. A silent warning passed between them. And again Six shivered, almost hearing the tuneless tinkle of an ice cream truck in her ears.

$$\oplus$$

AS BEN WALKED AWAY, a would-be assassin stared at his target. Waiting. Always waiting for the right moment. Excitement was building within him. Soon. The order was clear. Kill Hannah Winslow, no matter what the fallout.

He smiled at the thought. He'd enjoy watching her bleed. His body hardened at the thought of sweet Hannah begging for mercy. He imagined her naked in front of him, her blue eyes wide with pain and fear. He'd take his time, use his Ka-Bar Becker BK7 Combat knife to tear into her soft, tanned flesh. Hannah Winslow wouldn't be so high and mighty then.

He gave the knife strapped to his leg a tender caress.

He loved his job.

$$\oplus$$

BEN STARED AT THE phone in his hand, his mind racing. According to Paul Fuller, Addison and Benson had arrived on the island less than twenty-four hours ago. Their orders were clear.

Six had run out of time.

"I'm sorry, Ben," Paul said over the phone line thousands of miles away, locked away in the safety of his office on the eleventh floor. "I told Parker to hold off, that you had everything under control, but ...well, you understand."

Ben did understand.

It didn't make it any easier.

He hung up the phone and gazed across the lobby of the hotel. His eyes locked onto the beautiful yet deadly woman standing next to Ten. She smiled at something the kid said, her eyes lighting up. Ten blushed to the roots of his buzz cut hair.

"Not as sorry as I am," Ben whispered, reaching for his 9mm.

Chapter 31

~~

I'M GOING TO HAVE *to hurt and maybe even kill him, Six thought,* eyeing the man brushing his teeth in the bathroom mirror, a towel wrapped around his waist.

As if able to read her thoughts, Ben caught her eye and smiled, white foam rimming his lips like a rabid dog's. His wicked grin caused her stomach to clench.

Her eyes brimmed with tears. She blinked them away. Unless he let her go, one way or another, tomorrow one of them would be dead. She'd seen the look in his eyes earlier that afternoon. He looked … resigned … dangerous.

Something had happened and it didn't bode well for her continued heartbeat. For the rest of the evening he'd stayed quiet, watching her through lowered eyes.

Watching.

Always watching.

Waiting.

If Ben took a break from his babysitting duties, then Ten, still leery of her, had to do the job. He stood at least three feet behind her at all times. It drove her crazy.

How could she escape with these two dogging her every

step? She doubted Ben would leave her unprotected while she went scuba diving with Zach. So that left her with one choice: remove him from the equation.

Could she do it?

"Shower's all yours," Ben said from the bathroom doorway, now dressed in a pair of Levi's and a Rolling Stones T-shirt. She stared at the wide red lips pressed on the fabric. Lips pressed right above his heart.

One clean shot.

Her fingers trembled against the cold metal of the 9mm hidden beneath the folds of the bedspread.

It was the only way.

Against her will, she felt her eyes welling up, and a solitary tear slipped down her cheek. Ben crossed the room, his long legs eating up the physical distance between them.

He sat down on the bed next to her, his fingers brushing the blanket covered gun. But he didn't seem to know that's what it was. She released the trigger, blowing out a relieved breath.

"It's not that bad," he said, his voice deep, reassuring, and completely false.

Sadly they both knew it.

Yet the warmth of his body and the minty scent of mouthwash and spice swamped her senses. He was so close, more like the partner she once trusted with her life. Before she could stop her treacherous tongue, she blurted out, "I've made such a mess of everything. After ... Davis ...I wanted a fresh start."

He wrapped his arm around her, pulling her close. "I know, baby. If there was any other way—"

"You don't get it." She pushed him away, staring into his eyes, willing him to understand. "I can't escape."

"You've done a pretty damn good job so far." He rose from the bed and started to pace. "It took me almost six months to find you."

"That's not what I meant." She also rose, but instead of pacing, she stood in front of the full-sized mirror and stared into her own red-rimmed eyes. "I can't escape the fact that I took that shot. That I killed Davis."

He approached her from behind. Standing there, he looked so strong, so reassuring that she wanted nothing more than to lean into his strength. Then he spoke. "When Pillars is dead you can have your life back." He brushed his fingers along the slope of her neck. "Go back to where you belong, forget about Davis, about his death. All you need to do is tell me where Pillars is."

Liar, liar, she thought. Things would be much easier if she believed him, in him. But he'd burned her before, and she wasn't the kind of girl to let emotions rule her decisions.

Assassins didn't have such luxuries.

He spun her around, tilted her chin so that she faced him and held it there tenderly. Finally, his lips covered hers. The kiss started sweet and soft but quickly turned dangerous. Tongue met tongue, battling for supremacy in a war as old as time.

Man versus woman.

Killer versus killer.

The past raging against the uncertainty of the future.

She wrapped her arms around his neck, leaning into his strength, his power. His hands drifted down her body, roaming over her flesh, as his mouth did incredible things to her insides. Heat pooled in her stomach, spreading until she felt nothing but clawing, aching need.

When she was on the verge of giving into his gentle seduction, he dropped his hands and stepped away. His features hardened and his pupils became chips of ice. "Go take your shower," he said.

His implacable gaze told her exactly what she needed to know. Whatever was between them no longer mattered.

Ben would kill her.

He had new orders.

⊕

BEN STARED AT THE closed bathroom door, grinding his teeth. His body ached with need. More than ached. He considered kicking down the door and dragging a soapy, wet Six into his arms, making love to her until they both forgot their names, or in his case, finally remembered her real one.

Shaking his head to dispel the torturous thoughts, he crossed the room and jerked back the bedspread. Her 9mm sat on the cotton sheet, safety off, a round chambered. He narrowed his eyes. So she really did want him dead. Sadly that made him want her more. What had stopped her from killing him? Was she really an innocent victim as she claimed or a vicious traitor to her country? Did it matter anymore?

He picked up the 9mm, feeling the weight of it in the palm of his hand. So cold. Flipping the safety on, he pulled the magazine from the gun. The weapon looked so innocent sitting in the palm of his hand, but he knew just how deadly it could be, especially when wielded by his former partner.

He could attest to her skill with many weapons, from a stripped down 9mm to a crossbow in the middle of a war-torn desert. She knew how to kill. But Six, like Ben, wasn't quite sure how to live. If things were different, maybe, just maybe, they could learn.

Ben planned to make things a lot different.

For everyone.

Chapter 32

~

Halekulani Resort, Honolulu, HI
28Oct, 0800 hours

"I'm gonna order some coffee. Maybe a poached egg," Ten said, his innocent puppy-dog eyes sparkling with early morning excitement. "You want anything?"

Six smiled at Ten, grateful that the kid appeared to be thawing after the little 'drugging him' misunderstanding. Earlier he'd even offered to give her some privacy on her date with Zach after Ben assigned him the task of stalking her. Once Ben gave that order, he abruptly disappeared, after a flippant, "Have fun."

For some reason, Ben's words made her want to punch him in the throat. She should have been happy to be left in Ten's not-so-capable hands. At least she had a shot at carrying out her escape.

"Don't tell Agent Miller I left you alone," Ten was saying. "He wants me to stick with you all the time. But what fun's that on a date? And it's not like you're going anywhere, right?"

She quickly agreed, her smile as bright as the flowered-shirt Ten wore wrapped around his husky body. "Order me some green tea, please." She nodded to the hotel phone in Ten's hand. "Zach should be here in an hour, so you should have time for a full breakfast before we head to the boat."

As she said the word 'boat' a shiver ran up her spine. She hated boats, nearly as much as she disliked the ocean. Aircraft, no problem. Fast cars, piece of cake. Put her in a boat and the former assassin, a woman who'd base-jumped off the Eiffel Tower, turned four shades greener than Kermit the Frog.

But she had little choice in the matter. Her plan was set in motion a few hours before when she hired a sleek speedboat to meet her a mile from the dive site. She'd also paid a diver to leave an extra scuba tank in the deep waters of the wreck.

After spending a few minutes diving with Zach, she'd grab the extra tank and swim away to freedom. Once onboard the speedboat, she'd head for the nearest city and vanish amid the tourists. From there, changing identities and boarding a plane for an unknown locale would be child's play.

As long as Ben left her in Ten's hands.

"I'll order now," Ten said happily and went to call room service. Six smiled again. Poor Ben. The kid was a moron. He'd be lucky to survive his first mission. His naiveté was going to make her faking her death that much easier.

Especially if he got in her way.

Acid filled her throat at the thought. Killing Ten, or anyone for that matter, repulsed her. She'd lost her taste for death about the time Davis hit the ground, his brains and blood soaking into the cotton-candy stained concrete.

The memory of that day flashed through her mind. Pink fur and big bunny ears in her scope. The sun pounding down. The stench of sweat, fake beaver, and gym socks.

Ben's order to take the shot ….

A knock on the door roused her from her thoughts. Ten raised his hand, motioning her from the door and pulling his gun. Six shook her head. What assassin would knock on a hotel room door?

Idiot.

◈

TWO FLOORS DOWN, BEN thought the same thing about himself. Taking a sip from the ice-cold bottle of water in his hand rather than the whiskey he craved, he cursed himself a hundredth time for being such a fool.

Jealousy tore at his gut. Wanting Six was a bad idea. He'd known it from the first time his lips touched hers. Lips so sweet he wanted to kiss her forever. Those same lips that lied with ease. Those same lips that in an hour or so would be kissing that moron, Zach.

He shook his head. Six was his former partner. Nothing more. He had no say in what or who she did. Not that reminding himself of this did one bit of good. The thought of her in the arms of any man, let alone a douche like Zach, drove him crazy. So much so that Ben had stupidly left Ten in charge of her during her 'date' for fear of what Ben would do if Zach touched her.

Ben wanted things to go back to the way they had been. Back in Washington. With Six back to being his partner. Back to being the strong, dependable woman he'd believed her to be before he'd tasted her lying lips. Once they were back to business as usual, he'd be able to forget about her crooked smile, or the way she moaned his name when he touched her. He groaned, slamming his bottle of water on the bar.

What he needed was a nice long run to clear his head, to erase her from his mind. His short bark of laughter held little humor. "Like that will happen." Until he completed his mission, she would stay firmly in his head. He just hoped she'd stay the fuck out of his heart.

◈

THE KNOCK SOUNDED ON the hotel room door again. Gun in hand, Ten peered through the peephole. He shoved his weapon back in the holster at the small of his back and covered it with his ridiculous flowered shirt before opening the door.

A waiter pushed a cart with a teapot and a silver breakfast tray into the room. The scent of butter and bacon filled the air. The smell turned Six's stomach. She excused herself and headed for the bathroom to finish dressing for her 'date.'

What did you wear to fake your death?

A part of her felt guilty for using Zach. A bigger part hated the calculating look in Ben's eyes when he'd kissed her earlier. She shook her head. Ben would do whatever was necessary to get what he wanted, and at the moment, he wanted her to lead him to a killer. Sadly, Six wanted much more, from him and herself, which was why, once she escaped, she would never look back. The thought of never seeing Ben tore at her heart. But he'd made his move, and now she would make hers.

Placing her 9mm on the bathroom vanity she went to work on her makeup for her 'date.' For a woman who'd spent much of her life training to kill she knew little about the art of being a girl. All those girly skills other women seemed to learn as easily as their ABCs remained elusive to her. Styling hair and applying makeup still seemed way more complicated than the trickiest assassination scenario.

Most of the time her lack of feminine wiles didn't bother her; yet, over the last few days—since Ben reappeared in her life—she felt at a disadvantage. Was his passion all a lie or was Ben even mildly attracted to her? Could he fake passion for the sake of his mission? She shook off that thought, disgusted by her sudden insecurity. As a trained killer, she was above all that petty high school crap.

"Tea's ready," Ten called from the bedroom.

"I'll be right out," she said, running a mascara wand across her eyelashes and adding a touch of pink lipstick to her mouth.

She looked in the mirror and puckered her lips, which curled into a disgusted frown.

A second knock sounded at the door as she returned from the bathroom. *Zach's early*, she thought, hoping he wasn't planning on canceling. She needed to escape and quickly, before she lost her nerve. She wasn't sure how much longer she could be around Ben and not rip his Levi's off, even though he wanted her dead.

The asshole.

But then again, she'd never been good at picking Mr. Right. Mr. 'I'll Sleep with Your Neighbor While You're Away on a Business Trip,' sure, but Mr. Right remained elusive. Not that she was particularly interested in finding him.

Life was easier with a cat.

The knock sounded again. She detoured to answer the door, a welcoming smile on her face. The smile quickly faded, replaced by a sharp intake of breath as she focused on the .22 caliber pistol aimed at her heart.

Chapter 33

~

"HELEN?" SIX STEPPED BACK, her eyes on the barrel of the weapon in the older woman's steady hand. "What the—"

"Where's your friend Ben?" Helen asked, her small eyes darting around the hotel room like a ferret's.

Six held up her hands, disgusted by the fact that she'd not only let her assassin into the room to kill her, but that she had managed to leave her only weapon lying in the bathroom. These mistakes had sealed her fate. Fitting somehow.

Six backed up another step. "It's just you and me, Helen. No one else needs to get hurt." As she finished her statement, Ten lumbered into the hallway, looking big, dumb, and threatening. Her heart leapt into her throat.

"Tea's getting cold," he said, his eyes dancing from Six to the gun in Helen's hand. "Hey—"

Before he could finish his statement or go for the gun in his waistband, Six spun around and kicked him in the testicles. The force propelled him off his feet and to the ground, where he promptly rolled up into a ball. She winced as he hit the floor.

He cried out and then went silent as his eyes rolled back into his head.

Better sterile than dead, Six thought, but she doubted Ten would see it her way anytime soon. At least he was alive, and with luck, would remain that way.

Helen motioned to Ten with her gun. "Another little boy-toy, I see. What is it with women like you?"

"Forget about him." Six kept her voice relaxed. If, even for a second, Helen believed Ten was a threat, the baby-assassin would die. Six would do anything to stop that from happening. She had enough blood on her hands already. "He's no danger to you."

A smile spread over Helen's face, changing her plain features to almost pretty. "Let's go. We have a boat to catch." She motioned for Six to open the door and head into the corridor, keeping a safe distance between them.

A million possible scenarios filtered through Six's head, and not one of them ended well. Most ended with one or multiple bullet wounds. A chance Six wasn't prepared to take just yet.

Ben had taught her a lot in three years, and one of those lessons was, bide your time. So she would do just that. She walked down the hallway of the resort, her head held high while her heart slammed wildly in her chest.

Helen followed a few feet behind, the gun hidden in the folds of her drab sweater jacket. "Take the stairs," she said when Six paused at the elevators.

Six nodded, slowly moving to the stairwell, the same place she'd nearly died a day before. Had Helen waited in the darkened stairwell, gun and high-powered night vision goggles at the ready? Six shivered. The cold, concrete stairwell and the gun aimed at her back were taking their toll.

She briefly considered leaping over the edge of the stairs and free falling two stories to the concrete below. What was the worst that could happen? A broken femur?

Helen must've anticipated the possibility, for as soon as the heavy fire door closed, she fired her weapon into the darkened stairway below. "Don't even think about it," she said over the deafening retort. "Get moving." She shoved the gun into Six's spine. The warmth of the freshly fired weapon both soothed and terrified the former assassin.

Six started down the steps, catching Helen's reflection in the shiny handrail. Helen's smile was both smug and borderline insane.

One thing was for sure; Six wouldn't be faking her death.

Not today.

⊕

"Ten!" Ben grabbed the baby-assassin's shoulders, giving them a hard shake. "What the hell happened? Where's Six?"

Ten responded with a low moan. Ben shook him harder. "Come on, kid. Wake up." When Ten failed to return to a coherent state, Ben leapt up and prowled around the hotel suite, searching for any clue as to where Six went.

Damn her. She'd pulled her disappearing act one too many times. And now she had gone too far: she had injured Ten. When he found her she'd pay a stiff price for her deceit.

If he found her alive, he thought, catching sight of the 9mm on the bathroom vanity. A lump formed in his throat. He grabbed the house phone. "Room 214," he said into the receiver. "I need to see the surveillance video for the last hour." He paused, his eyes flickering over to Ten, who had managed to crawl to his knees, his hands between his legs. "Oh, and ice. Lots of ice."

Chapter 34

Pacific Ocean, Latitude 21.042808, Longitude 157.890015
28Oct, 0900 hours

WAVES SMASHED INTO THE fiberglass side of the speedboat as Helen steered the Sea Ray through the island channel. Her gun remained carefully trained on Six even in these rough waters.

Six gripped the side of the boat, her stomach roiling with each six-foot wave. She disliked the ocean. A lot. If Ben had recalled that fact, it might have clued him in on Six's plot to fake her death. A moot point now. Death, not the faked kind, appeared a real possibility.

The longer and deeper Helen steered the boat into the sun-drenched waters, the worse the odds for Six's survival. She would die, here, today, at the hands of a killer CPA.

Son-of-a-number-crunching-bitch.

Her mind rebelled at the thought. She wouldn't go out without a fight. Helen would regret killing her. Six would damn well make sure of that.

The coastline faded from view as Helen cut the engine. The

boat went slack in the water, waves battering the hull like a heavy metal drummer. Island gulls cried a mournful song, reminding Six of her adventure on the beach and the sweet kiss she'd shared with Ben. *He'll find me*, she thought, both encouraged and horrified at the idea. Would Helen kill him too? Would she get some kind of assassin's two-for-one deal?

Six closed her eyes against the salty spray of the ocean waves and silently prayed that for once Ben would abandon his mission and just walk away.

⊕

THE MISSION WAS THE furthest thing from Benjamin Miller's mind. His only thoughts were of finding Six. He'd spent the last twenty minutes reviewing the resort's security footage for any sign of her, all the while questioning a less than happy Ten.

"She kicked me in the nuts," Ten complained, not for the first time in the last half-hour. He gripped a large bag of ice to his crotch, his face regaining a little of its color.

Ben shook his head, his eyes steady on the surveillance monitor. "She saved your life."

Ten frowned as he had the last five times Ben had repeated the statement, "I could've taken the old lady."

Sadly Ben knew how untrue that was. There was no doubt in his mind Six had saved Ten's life. A fact he was extremely thankful for. The sheer amount of dead-partner paperwork would've kept him buried for the next month. Not to mention that Ben wasn't about to lose another partner. Not today. That included Six. He would find her.

⊕

HELEN STARED AT THE deep blue ocean, her hand steady on the gun as if it was an extension of her body. She knew exactly what she had to do. Faces swarmed through her mind. Some might call them victims, but Helen knew the truth. Linda Burke must die. It was for the best. Surely Linda would realize that.

⊕

"WHERE IS THAT DAMN case report?" Ben slammed his hand on the desk. The sound reverberated around the small office like a gunshot. The resort security guard winced as his paper cup bounced once and fell over, spilling the last drops of his morning coffee across the wooden desk.

The guard lifted the cup, mopped the liquid with a crumpled napkin, and threw both items in the trash. "Sir, the mainland detective said it would take twenty minutes to scan and email the report over. That was only ten minutes ago."

Ben ran his hand through his black hair, trying to calm his racing heart. Six was out there somewhere with a killer, a drably dressed and extremely boring killer, but one hired by Pillars to kill her nonetheless. To make matters worse, Ben had no clue where to find them.

The resort security footage, along with Ten's description of the early morning events, proved one thing: Helen Smith wasn't who she appeared to be. So far, a search with the FBI turned up nothing on a Helen Smith in San Diego. The San Diego PD was a different story. They had five unsolved murder cases in the city over the last three years with one common thread—Helen Smith. Would Six be her sixth? The irony wasn't lost on Ben. Not if he could help it.

On Ben's orders, Ten had searched Helen's hotel suite, finding nothing of use, with the exception of a digital camera with photos that featured Six on the volcano hike a few days earlier. Helen must've been stalking her, lying in wait for the chance to take a shot.

The fear clogging Ben's throat increased as minutes ticked by. Helen wasn't some amateur. If Six wasn't fish food already, she soon would be, while he sat on his ass doing nothing to stop it.

He jumped out of his chair, sending it flying across the small security station. "I have to find her," he said to Ten. "Stay here and wait for the cops. Fill them in on what we've got as soon as they get here."

Without another word, Ben ran for the door. He wouldn't lose Hannah Winslow again.

⊕

"How much, Helen?" Six asked over the sound of the ocean waves pounding against the hull. The boat rocked violently under her feet, making her seasick as well as heartsick. Helen, however, didn't appear to be bothered by the rocky motion as she kept her weapon trained on Six. Six repeated her question, "How much are you being paid?"

Helen frowned, a deep wrinkle creasing her forehead. "I don't see how that's relevant to our current situation."

Six laughed. "Oh, it's relevant all right." She took a step forward, her voice rising over the crash of the surf. "I want to know just how much my life is worth to OPS. Twenty thousand? Fifty?" Six doubted the price on her head was much higher, not with the cheapskate Parker Langdon at the helm. He had once asked Ben for an accounting of every bullet used in the assassination of an African warlord.

Helen's uninspired eyes darted back and forth. "OPS?"

Now it was Six's turn to frown. "You aren't working for OPS?" When Helen shook her head, Six took another step closer, her face twisting with confusion and anger. "Just who the hell do you work for?"

Assassins were bound to pick up an enemy or two. Over the course of her career, Six had managed to accumulate a few. Ben had a few more. It came with the job. The idea of dying at the hands of a CPA hired by some unknown enemy pissed her off even more than being offed by her own people.

She shook her head, running through the list of people who wanted her dead. One name popped out. After all, he'd tried to kill her at least once when he blew up Ben's Jeep. "*Who*, Helen? John Pillars?" she demanded, stabbing her finger toward the drab and now pink-faced woman.

Helen retreated a step, her back against the gunwale. "You know damn well who I work for, Linda," she said, her words fading into the tropical breeze. "Zach."

Chapter 35

~~

Halekulani Resort, Honolulu, HI
28 Oct, 0900 hours

THE MAN IN QUESTION, Zachary Coleman Barber, moved toward Ben, his hands fisted at his sides. "Looking for someone?" he asked with a sneer.

Ben ignored him, his mind focused on retracing Helen's steps. She must have left some sort of clue as to her plan. Assassinations took preparation. This one was no different, except that it was. Six was the target. His partner. His Six. The woman he'd vowed to protect until death did they part. And Ben was far from ready to part.

Fear nearly robbed the once controlled and deadly assassin of his ability to reason. Much to his dismay, he was going insane at the thought that this very moment might be Six's last.

Zach gave a small laugh. "I see how desperate you are for her, but you won't win. Not this time."

Zach's words finally penetrated Ben's mind. Was Zach somehow involved? Was he working with Helen? Was he a part of a hit team sent by Pillars? It made sense, Ben supposed—a couple of killers hiding behind a false front of liquid refreshment.

Ben spun around to face Zach, his fist catching him in the right lung. Zach dropped to the sandy walkway with a surprised gasp. "Where is she?" Ben asked, his voice more lethal than his fist.

"Who?" Zach squeezed out, his lungs squeaking like a leaky balloon.

"Six."

Zach gave him a blank look.

"Hannah. Linda. Whatever she calls herself." He tapped Zach on the back of the head. "If Helen hurts her, I will rip you to pieces. Do you understand?"

Zach tried to push Ben away, but Ben shoved him back down onto the heated sand. "What are you talking about?" Zach asked, sucking air through his teeth as he struggled to a sitting position. "What's going on? Why would Helen hurt Linda? We're a team. Team H2. And nothing you can offer Linda can change that."

Ben punched him in the kidney.

Zach's bravado cracked when Ben raised his fist again. "Wait," Zach said, warding off another blow. This time Ben allowed him to stand. "Did something happen with Linda and Helen? When I saw them together this morning Linda was acting strange and she cancelled our scuba trip, and then Helen looked … I didn't think anything of it—"

Ben grabbed the lapel of Zach's polo shirt, unsure if he believed him until tears gathered in Zach's pretty blue eyes. No assassin would burst into tears after a few puny hits. Disgusted, Ben twisted the fabric until it choked the smaller man. "Where were they going?"

"I have no idea," Zach cried, snot bubbling from his nose.

"Think." Ben pulled tighter. Zach's eyes began to bulge like a cartoon character's. "Were they headed toward the beach or to the parking lot?"

Zach's eyebrows narrowed in concentration as if this single question might be his last. And by the look in Ben's eyes, it might. "Toward the dock, I think, but I can't be sure. My company rented a motorboat for the week. Maybe Helen was taking Linda sightseeing."

$\oplus$

SOMETHING WASN'T ADDING UP. Helen kept referring to her as Linda Burke, H2 marketing whiz, not as Six, former government-contracted bunny killer. Great news for Six, not so great for her alias, Linda Burke, in that, Helen clearly wanted Linda dead.

The fact that she wanted Linda dead proved one thing, that Helen wasn't a trained assassin hired by OPS or John Pillars, merely an amateur with delusions of grandeur. The odds of Six's continued survival increased a few degrees.

Or so she thought until Helen tossed her a rope and ordered her to tie her hands together. Pretending to comply, she slowly twisted the heavy rope around her wrists, while leaving enough slack to make an easy escape. Once her hands were tied, Helen nodded, taking the rope in one hand and yanking it tight.

Unfortunately Helen wasn't as new to this game as Six first suspected. Her heartbeat increased at the realization. "What's this all about, Helen?" she asked the older woman, stalling for time as she calculated the best way to avoid a bullet to the head.

If she could distract Helen long enough, she could make a break for it. But where would she go? The ocean seemed like the logical choice, for a stronger swimmer. Seeing as her skills in the water equaled a fish's on land, swimming to safety wasn't the best option. "Did I forget to turn in October's expense report?"

"October's report isn't due for two weeks," Helen replied automatically.

Six tried to contain her smile. Cold-blooded killer aside, the true Helen was as predictable as tax season. "So what's with the gun then?"

Helen seemed to shrink within herself, her drab brown clothing sucking away what little life was inside her. "I didn't want it to come to this," she waved the gun toward Six, "but you left me with no choice."

"There's always a choice." Six lowered her eyes, thinking of her own past mistakes. Faces that often haunted her nightmares flipped through her brain like a vindictive Rolodex, ending on the image of bloody pink bunny ears. Davis. Her heart gave a squeeze, but she ignored the pain. "You just have to make the right one. It doesn't have to end this way."

Helen snorted, both bitter and repulsed. "Who are you to lecture me on morals? You disgust me. You're nothing but a whore, seducing every man you see." She jabbed the gun at Six. "Just like the others. Well, I'll tell you this," her face contorted, "I won't let you have him."

Six held up her tied hands to calm the older, clearly insane woman. "Hold on," she said, trying to understand what Helen was blabbing on about. "You won't let me have who? Ben? But you hardly know him."

Helen screeched with frustration. "Zach! Damn it. You can't have Zach."

Six wrinkled her nose. It was her turn to be disgusted. "What makes you think I want *him*?"

"Don't you dare deny it," Helen said, her face turning red, but not from the burning sun. "I saw the two of you together at the volcano. You seduced him. But let me tell you, it won't work. Zach is mine. He's always been mine and always will be. He loves me." She paused in her tirade, her eyes growing moist. "He sometimes gets distracted by hussies like you, but he always comes back to me. I'm his soul mate. And I won't let you destroy what we have together."

Six tilted her head. "Have you mentioned this to Zach? Because I'm not so sure he'd agree."

Her words, meant to infuriate the mad woman into losing control, had the opposite effect. Helen steadied the gun. "Laugh all you want, Linda. But your time with H2 is over." Her finger flexed on the trigger. "You're fired!"

The peaceful ocean air exploded with the sound of a single gunshot, followed by a woman's scream.

Chapter 36

~~

Bᴇɴ's ʜᴇᴀʀᴛ sʟᴀᴍᴍᴇᴅ ᴡɪʟᴅʟʏ in his chest as he shot through the choppy ocean waters at forty-four knots. Wind whipped the stern, making steering nearly impossible. But speed was what he needed most. The salty spray stung his cheeks and raised tears that clouded his vision, but he didn't slow down. Not with Six's life in his hands.

Ahead on the port side he made out a tiny speck in the vast blue of ocean. A small, insignificant dot. He could only hope the dot was Helen's speedboat, and that Six was still aboard, alive.

For once in his life, Benjamin Miller, cold-blooded assassin, felt genuine terror, the kind of terror that stole a man's breath away. The kind that turned his knees and resolve to jelly. What if he was too late? What if Six, at this very moment, lay drowning in a pool of her own blood?

White knuckled, he pushed the speedboat even faster.

⊕

Sɪx sᴛʀᴜɢɢʟᴇᴅ ꜰᴏʀ ʙʀᴇᴀᴛʜ as an unbearable weight dragged

her deeper and deeper into its warm embrace. She fought for air with every bit of strength left in her oxygen-deprived lungs, kicking with her last ounce of energy.

She pictured Ben's face, his humor-filled eyes and quick easy smile. How she longed to see him one last time, to tell him how sorry she was for everything, to tell him how she had really felt that day she left OPS, left him.

His face swam above her as if she'd conjured him out of the salty ocean air. "Ben?" she managed to call out before a wave toppled her, dragging her back into the depths of the ocean.

She wrapped her tied hands around Helen's unconscious body and waited as the current swallowed them, knocking them back down into the dark blue depths of the salty ocean.

Trying to stay upright, to measure the distance to the surface and fresh, clean air, she fought the current, but the waves were in control, pulling her this way and that.

The only thing she could do was hold onto the woman who'd tried to shoot her and pray. Deeper and deeper the watery depths dragged the two women down until darkness obscured her vision. Blood pounded in her ears, growing slower and slower as the oxygen in her bloodstream depleted.

Then, as suddenly as the wave swallowed her, the undertow released her from its grip. Freed, she used the last of her strength to kick to the surface for what might be the last time. Her lungs burned, threatening to explode. Her limbs grew heavy, so heavy she could barely move them.

Sunlight and oxygen shimmered twenty feet overhead.

Fifteen feet.

Ten.

Grayness seeped into her vision. *I'm not going to make it*, she thought. But rather than her life flashing before her eyes, she saw only one image.

Ben.

Franticly Ben pressed his mouth to hers, blowing every ounce of breath from his lungs into her withered ones. Then he wrapped his muscular arms around her and Helen, kicking to the surface.

When the trio broke through the waves, he dragged the women to his speedboat, careful to avoid the heated propeller. He pulled himself onto the stern and then hoisted the unconscious wannabe-killer aboard before yanking Hannah from the salty water.

Taking her in his arms, his body shaking with adrenaline and horrible images of what might've been, he held her tightly against his chest, running his hands along her body to check for injuries. Finding none, his heart rate returned to normal and he slowly pulled away. Their eyes locked and for a moment nothing else mattered. Not her betrayal. Not his mission. Not the killer coughing up water a few feet away.

Ben smiled down at the beautiful but bedraggled assassin in his arms. "Nice day for a swim."

Chapter 37

~~

Pacific Ocean, Latitude 21.7834, Longitude 156.27315
28Oct, 1000 hours

Six shivered in the bright sunlight, her clothing stiff and still damp from her dip in the ocean. Helen sat a few feet away, her arms tied to the anchor with thick, heavy rope.

Ben steered the speedboat to shore, keeping one eye on the water and the other on Six. The emptiness in her eyes scared him more than anything else. She looked defeated. Ben wasn't about to let that stand. "Ten sends his best," he said over the whine of the engine.

Her lips curved into a half-smile. "I'll bet." She winced, remembering the look on his face as his testicles ascended. "I hope I didn't hurt him too badly."

Ben smiled and shrugged. "He definitely learned a lesson about pretty girls. I doubt you'll get a chance to kick him a second time. He might shoot you if you even look at him funny." Slowing the speedboat, he turned to face her, his gaze intent. "Are you ready to tell me what happened back there?" He motioned to Helen's abandoned boat and the ocean waves that had nearly cost Six her life.

As long as he lived, he would not forget the terror he felt as the waves swept her under for what he believed would be the last time. Why the hell was she in the water in the first place? Six hated the ocean. She'd insisted as much enough times that only an idiot would forget it.

She wiped a lock of wet hair from her eyes and glared at Helen, who glared right back. "Helen had a little mishap." At his raised eyebrow, she continued, "She tried to shoot me in the head, but the gun was kicked out of her hand."

"And then you decided to go for a swim?" he asked with a frown.

"Something like that."

Helen screeched, "She tried to drown me."

He spun toward Helen, his face so cold the older woman immediately shut up. To Six, he said, "I take it you did a little more than kick the gun from her hand."

She crossed her arms under her breasts, giving him an excellent view of the outline of her nipples through the thin fabric of her T-shirt. He valiantly tried to look away, but his gaze couldn't help but return to her chest.

She glanced down, quickly dropping her arms. "I was a wee bit annoyed by Helen's trying to put a bullet in me so I might've used a little more force than necessary. She fell overboard." She paused and gave a little shrug. "Not really my fault at all."

He grinned. "Why the hell did you jump in to save her? You should've left her for the sharks."

She gave a violent shiver at the mention of the man-eating predators roaming the ocean. "I felt bad."

"She tried to kill you!" He looked as if he might throw Helen overboard just for the hell of it.

"But she didn't succeed." Six grinned, recalling a mantra Ben often told her while on a mission to yet another hellhole in a war-torn country run by yet another greedy dictator responsible for the massacre of his own people. "A semi-wise man once told me, 'It's not the intent that matters but the end result.' I believe that."

He raised an eyebrow. "*Semi*-wise, huh?"

"He has his moments," she said with a shrug.

"You still should've let her drown." He glared at Helen. "Save the taxpayers some money."

"What's that supposed to mean?" Six tilted her head to stare at the seemingly fragile, timid woman. Helen responded by lashing out with her right foot, narrowly missing Six's knee.

Without a word, Ben yanked Helen to her feet and tossed her into the back of the boat, where she landed with a loud thud. "You were saying?" he asked Six, once Helen's screeches subsided.

She paused, tilting her head to one side. "For a killer, Helen really does have terrible aim. She tried to shoot me twice, missed both times. And this time I was less than three feet away. It's sort of sad really."

He laughed. "So it was her at the volcano?"

"Not very professional, I know," she shrugged, "but apparently Helen called dibs on Zach and took offense at his growing interest in yours truly." When Ben's smile grew, she quickly added, "A pity. I really think Zach and I could have something special."

"Over my dead body," he said, the smile quickly leaving his face.

She felt guilty for teasing Ben. After all, he had saved her life less than twenty minutes ago. "I'm kidding. But I do feel a little sorry for him."

"Don't be. He will get along just fine." He looked over at Helen, who spat out a string of curse words. "Isn't she a treat?"

"She's a woman scorned." Six grinned. "Something you know a little about."

"Very little." He frowned. "But before you get to feeling too sorry for sweet, old scorned Helen, you'll be interested to know the cops in San Diego are looking for her. She's a suspect in five separate murder charges."

"Five?" Her voice raised two octaves. "All women Zach dated?"

He nodded. "He does have a way with the ladies."

Chapter 38

〰

BEN AND SIX SPENT the better part of the rest of the afternoon at a police substation telling and retelling their story to a pair of detectives. At first the cops didn't even try to mask their disbelief, but once they began interrogating Helen, they quickly changed their minds.

Helen admitted to shooting at Six at the volcano, and later, trying to run the hotel van off the road. Both acts were a response to Zach's mounting interest in the other woman. After Ben arrived on scene, Helen stopped her attacks.

Until today.

Which meant one thing.

There was a second assassin on the loose, a man with a crazed laugh and one goal, to kill Hannah Winslow.

⊕

HOURS LATER, BEN AND Six found themselves alone in the resort elevator on the way to her hotel room. Six closed her eyes for a second, leaning back against the elevator wall. "I just want to fall into bed and never get out."

Ben cleared his throat. "Maybe I should keep you company." He waggled his eyebrows with an exaggerated leer. "After all, who knows what kind of trouble you might find yourself in?"

"True," she said, lowering her gaze to his invitingly warm lips. "Perhaps you could check under the bed for boogiemen?"

"No way." He gave an affected shudder. "Dust bunnies terrify me."

At his words her eyes quickly lost their teasing glint. Her mind flashed back to bloodstained bunny ears. And the man inside the mask. She stepped back, distancing herself from the man she was coming closer and closer to falling for, if only he'd trust her.

"Six ..." he said, as if reading her thoughts.

The plea in his voice was her undoing, even if it was all a lie. Nearly dying had a weird way of putting one's life in perspective. At that moment nothing but touching and being touched mattered. She catapulted herself into his arms and kissed him with everything she had to give.

He staggered under her assault, but quickly overcame his surprise and held his ground, kissing her back with equal if not greater desperation and frustration. He truly did want her, the hard length of him told her that much. Her fingers caressed him through the fabric of his jeans. He groaned as their tongues played a quick and dirty game of tag.

He pressed her back against the wall of the elevator, her bottom hitting the emergency stop on the console. The elevator shuddered to a rest but neither assassin noticed. Six wrapped her legs around him, her body quivering with liquid need.

His hot mouth trailed wet kisses along the curve of her jaw, down her neck, and over the swells of her breasts. "You'll be the death of me," he whispered, his breathing coming in hard, short gasps.

She abruptly pulled back as the truth of his words settled into her heart, forming a lump of fear in her stomach. She wouldn't let him die for her. "Just tonight," she said, the words expressing equal parts promise and warning. "Tomorrow we forget this ever happened."

Ben seemed to want to argue, but her hand on the fly of his Levis quickly distracted him.

⊕

Minutes later she slid her key card through the magnetic reader on the door-lock, watching as the red light beeped green. Ben's hands roamed over her body, scorching her with each caress. She spun around, her mouth locking on his in a heated embrace.

"Oh God, Six," he said against her ravenous mouth.

"Take me," she whispered.

"Oh baby, I plan on it. I don't care if the room blows up again." He pressed his erection against her flat stomach, feeling the muscles clench in response. "Nothing is keeping me from having you."

"You have your orders, soldier."

Moments later, Ben's Henry Rollin's Band T-shirt disappeared, along with his brain's ability to function. He had one single-minded purpose now, to see Hannah Winslow naked. Nothing else mattered. Not John Pillars. Not OPS. Not the past or the future. Not anything.

With one little exception.

The dead waiter on the hotel room floor.

Chapter 39

THIS CANNOT BE HAPPENING, Six thought as the paramedics wheeled the gurney from her hotel room. They bumped the edge of the door, causing the dead man to bounce like a leaking beach ball. She closed her eyes and counted to ten. When she opened them, nothing had changed. Her room was still swarming with cops and crime scene technicians and stinking of dead waiter and spoiled food.

Ben entered the room once the paramedics left, a grim smile on his lips. He handed her a steaming coffee in a cardboard cup, the heat helping to still the shivering caused by the shock of seeing a dead man in her hotel room. Ben was saying, "The M.E. thinks the guy had a heart attack."

"But we know better."

"Yeah. Poison is my guess." He stroked his chin, as if running through a list of possible poisons. "Probably a fast-acting neurotoxin." An assassin standard. He'd used his fair share over the years.

Her eyes narrowed on the room service tray from this morning. The one Ten had ordered right before Helen arrived at the door. "Looks like Ten owes me for saving his life yet again."

He followed her glance. "How so?"

"The assassin poisoned our breakfast, either the tea or the food." She stopped, weighing her words. "The waiter came to take the food tray. It's past his lunchtime. He's hungry so he takes a little bite. Bam, he's dead." She swallowed hard, thinking of what could've happened if Helen hadn't kidnapped her. Or if Ben had stuck around this morning for breakfast. Too many innocent people had died already. She couldn't bear the thought of someone else dying because of her, especially Ben.

"It wasn't your fault," Ben said, reaching for her hand, but she quickly pulled away.

"No, it wasn't." Her gaze settled on him as she said the words. "We both know who's responsible."

"John Pillars—"

"OPS—" she said at the same time.

"You can't honestly think I had anything to do with this," he said, throwing up his hands. "I'm not the 'kill an innocent waiter' kind of guy."

"Not you." She gave a bitter laugh. "Not directly. But someone at OPS. The same someone who put Davis inside that suit, and then tried to blow us up."

"Six—"

"I'm not a traitor, Ben. I've never met John Pillars, and I sure as hell didn't purposely kill Davis." She swallowed past the lump in her throat. "I need you to believe me. To trust me. The rabbit hole goes deeper than we know, and until we figure out who is pulling the strings, no one is safe."

Silence met her plea.

"Message received," she said, turning from him before he could see the tears running down her cheeks.

He reached for her hand. She flinched when his fingers wrapped around her arm, as if she couldn't stomach his touch.

He dropped his hand, freeing her. She rose from the bed and crossed the room, vanishing through the open door without looking back.

Chapter 40

~~

AFTER SIX LEFT HER hotel room, Ben motioned for Ten to follow her. He wasn't sure anymore if he was protecting her or protecting himself from her, but he needed time alone, time to think, to reassess.

Two hours later, after the detectives and forensic personnel left her hotel room, now a crime scene, Ben knocked on Ten's door. "Six, I know you're in there. Let me in so we can talk."

No answer.

"Open this door," he demanded.

⊕

TEN RUBBED HIS CHIN. "What should I do?"

"Open that door and you'll walk bow-legged for the rest of your days," Six said, rising to her feet. Her mind raced with possible escape routes and plans, all of which seemed ridiculous now.

As much as she wanted to run, to disappear forever, she would never be free from Benjamin Miller. He was like a big chocolate bar. You knew in your heart of hearts that it was no good for you, but you couldn't help but devour the whole thing. Well, she'd taken a bite, and instead of the sweetness she'd expected, there are only bitterness.

"Ten—" she began, only to be interrupted by Ben's appearance at the glass doors of the patio, glass doors that happened to be two stories up.

Ben tugged at the door, which slid open easily in his hands. She knew just how those damn doors felt. All it took was for him to touch her, and she opened. "You could've knocked," she said, motioning to the door in the main room.

"I did. I guess you couldn't hear me." He glanced over at the baby-assassin sitting awkwardly on the couch, a bag of ice covering his swollen junk. "Beat it," he motioned to the door.

"But it's my room," Ten whined, petulant as a child. "I just ordered a steak. I'm starving. I haven't had anything to eat since this morning." He punctuated his comment with a glare at Six.

She shot him a sweet, innocent smile in return.

Pulling out his wallet, Ben handed the kid a hundred dollar bill. "Have a nice dinner on me." His tone did not allow for any arguments. "In the restaurant downstairs."

"But—"

Ben's eyes wandered to the beautiful killer standing a few feet away, her hands on her hips. "A really long dinner. Maybe take in a show." Ben helped Ten to his feet, walking/shoving him across the room. With his free hand Ben unlatched the deadbolt and tossed Ten out the door.

"Have a nice night," Six said as the door closed in the baby-assassin's round face. Once Ben latched the deadbolt, he slowly turned to her. "What's left to say?" she asked, a little tremble of sadness in her voice.

He crossed the room in three strides, his mouth effectively cutting off her words. He kissed her with tsunami-like passion, unbridled and all consuming. He swept her off her feet, and before she knew what hit her, she was lying flat on her back on Ten's bed. Ben leaned over her, his knee between her thighs.

Brushing a wayward lock of hair from her eyes, he grinned down at her. "Words are overrated, don't you think?"

Again, before she could form a coherent string of words, his mouth took possession. His predatory tongue circled hers, zeroing in on its prey.

Angry enough to want to cause him physical pain, she knocked him to the bed, straddling his legs. She didn't, however, break their kiss. He responded by nipping at her lower lip, slowly drawing it into his mouth. His callused trigger finger brushed the sensitive skin of her throat, moving lower across her heated flesh.

"I still hate you," she lied, her hands bunching in the fabric of his T-shirt, pulling at the offending garment. "This changes nothing."

He grinned, and in one quick motion, yanked the shirt over his head and tossed it onto the floor. Six's own T-shirt, shorts, and panties soon followed. Straddling her former partner while wearing nothing but a black lace bra somehow felt so right, even as his hot gaze promised a wealth of naughtier things to come. "I know," he answered, sounding totally unconcerned.

Lifting his head, he brushed his hot and hard mouth over her lace-clad nipple. Heat pooled at her center, growing in intensity as he undid her bra with one hand while claiming her breast with his tongue. Throwing her head back, she allowed his sweet assault to continue until she was ready for much more.

'More' was delightfully unpredictable, she soon learned, as he once again claimed control, tossing her on her back as he stripped off his jeans and underwear. She drank in the sight of his perfect body, her gaze fixed on his erection.

"Keep looking at me like that and this will be over before we get to the good stuff," he said, his eyes blazing with heat and hunger, like a wild animal preparing for a feast.

With effort she tore her eyes away. "Let's see what you got."

More than up for the task and damn good at following orders,

Ben dropped down on the bed, his body parting her thighs. His mouth started with her breast and trailed downward to her molten center.

At the first taste, Six was nearly jolted off the bed as the waves of orgasm surprised her in their intensity. Her toes curled and she screamed.

He swallowed her cries with his mouth, entering her as her body convulsed around his erection. She had to give him credit—he tried to hold back, to take things slow—but she wanted none of that. This was all about sex and rage.

Punishment and promise.

Not love.

She dug her fingers into his back, pushing him harder and deeper inside her. Her second orgasm shook her already rattled body, tilting the world around her until all thoughts were erased, and hot, excited sensation took control.

Once the tremors of pleasure subsided to mere earth-shaking, she regained control of the situation, forcing him onto his back while she took the lead. Ben appeared more than happy to hand over the reigns as she drove him to the edge and over it.

As he came he shouted her name. Her real name.

Hannah.

Chapter 41

~~

LATER THAT NIGHT, AS Six lay asleep in his arms, Ben pulled a small needle from the nightstand drawer. Inside the needle was a black dot with enough computer power to track anyone anywhere in the world. He kissed the back of Six's neck, enjoying her soft moan. His hands shook as he stared at the tracking device and back at her soft skin. Her quick intake of breath convinced him of what he needed to do.

He would not lose her. Not now. Not ever again. Unwilling to question his motives too closely or his feelings for the woman lying in his arms, he trailed his fingers down her spine. Closing his eyes, he pressed the needle to the swell of her hip to where the inky outline of dolphins frolicking sat on her flesh, took a deep steady breath, and injected the tracker under her skin.

She jerked awake, her eyes flying to his.

He glanced away.

"Bastard," she whispered. In one fluid motion, she launched herself from the bed and dashed into the bathroom.

The only signs of his treachery were the empty needle in his hand and a small spot of blood on the sheet, not to mention the furious assassin just beyond the bedroom door.

Ben dropped back on the pillows. To her this would be yet another betrayal at his hands. One more sign that he'd never trust her. One more reason to hate him.

⊕

FOR THE NEXT FEW hours, Six refused to speak to Ben, his latest duplicity fresh in her mind and embedded under her skin. Try as she might, she could not remove the tracking device. At one point she'd dug at it with a six-inch knife, but no luck. The damn thing taunted her, just below the surface of her skin, unreachable, much like her former partner. Her heart gave a squeeze at the thought.

Eventually her body would reject the invading device, just as she should've done last night. *Damn him*.

For the rest of the afternoon, when she inevitably ran into Ben in the resort lobby or the elevator, or even at the beach, he acted as if nothing had happened. He'd merely nodded and moved on, evasive tactics that had kept him alive for the past couple of hours. Ten stayed at her side on Ben's orders, but Ben stayed elusive.

On top of everything, she grew more desperate with each passing minute to leave the island and her former partner. Somewhere another assassin lurked, one much more skilled than Helen. He would make his move soon, and someone would die. Because of her. Again.

"Stop following me around like a lost puppy. It's creeping me out." She gave Ten a shove to emphasize her words. He quickly cupped his manly parts and jumped back. She winced, feeling guilty. The thought of Ten dying because of her sharpened her tone even more. "I'm not going anywhere"—*much to my dismay*, she thought—"so back the fuck off." She plopped down in a pool-side recliner and yanked open a magazine.

Mostly, she wanted Ten as far away from her as possible, just in case. Besides, why have her followed when Ben could find her with the flip of a switch? The thought made her angry, and terrified, all over again.

What a fool she was. Ben had never trusted her and he never would. Disgusted with herself, she closed her eyes, because, despite everything he'd done—every time he betrayed her or used her for his precious mission—she couldn't stop thinking about him, about the feel of his hands on her body, about the way his lips curved into a half-smile when he thought she wasn't watching.

As if having conjured him up, she opened her eyes and there he stood, in all his slouching, rumpled, gorgeous splendor. His black hair shone in the bright tropical sunlight and his eyes flashed with humor and something else, something that made her insides tighten.

"Beat it, kid. The grownups need to talk," he said to Ten before facing Six. Not waiting for Ten to follow his order, Ben handed her a small paper bag. "Here."

Her eyes narrowed, but when he didn't say anything more, she opened the bag and removed an eight-ounce bottle of sunscreen. When she glanced up at him for an explanation, he shrugged. "I wanted to buy you a 'Thanks for last night and I'm sorry about this morning' card but the hotel shop was all out."

He dropped down next to her, grabbing the sunscreen from her hands. Pouring a healthy amount into his palm, he began to rub it on her shoulders. "So it was either sunscreen or a tube of toothpaste—minty fresh, mind you—means of apology. I made an executive decision and went with option number one."

"How bold of you." She rolled onto her stomach, enjoying the feel of his hands on her skin much more than she should've. "What exactly are you sorry for?"

Ben winced. "The tracking device?"

She rolled her eyes. "That sounded more like a question than an apology. Why don't you try again?"

"Fine," he said with a drawn out sigh. He reached for her

arms and pulled her body to his, "I'm—," he began, only to be interrupted by a large shadow falling across the two assassins.

"Sorry to interrupt," Ten said. A flush of dull red stained his face from shaved head to chin.

"Then don't," Ben growled.

"What is it, Curtis?" Six asked, her voice sweet in contrast to the promise of violence in Ben's gaze.

Ten shot her a smile of appreciation before stammering something about the police, a phone call, and the other side of the island. The only words Six clearly understood were 'dead' and 'waiter.'

Ben quickly rose to his feet. "Say that again."

Ten repeated his explanation, slower this time. "One of the Hawaii detectives called. Ocha or something. I couldn't make out his name." At Ben's frown, the kid rushed on, "Anyway he said to tell you that you were right about the waiter being poisoned."

"Damn," Ben said, sparing Six a small glance.

Ten wasn't finished. "They got lucky, he said. They traced the poison to a shop on the other side of the island." Ten passed Ben a piece of hotel stationery. "This is the address to the shop. The detective said for you to meet him there." Ten reached into his pocket and pulled out a set of keys. "The valet pulled your Jeep around."

A smile spread over Ben's face, a smile that chilled Six to the core. It was the same smile he wore just before an assassination. A killer smile.

"Ben—" Six began, but he cut her off.

"Relax. Everything's going to be fine. I'll be back in less than an hour and we'll finish what we started." Which sounded much more like a threat than a promise to her ears. "Ten, take care of her."

Ten nodded like an eager puppy. "Yes, sir."

Six rolled her eyes. Ben grinned before he bent down,

grabbed her chin in his hand, and kissed the breath out of her. "For luck."

She pulled away, staring into his eyes. Words she would never say rose in her throat, but she choked them down. "I hate you, but I'll be pissed if you die. Got it?"

He shrugged. "Don't worry about me. I'm bulletproof." He paused. "You won't leave?"

She nodded.

"You promise?"

She nodded again. "I'm done running, Ben. I promise."

"Good." With that final word, he kissed her once more, and then walked away. About a hundred feet away, he stopped, turning back as if he wanted to say something. Instead of speaking, he raised his hand, forming a gun with his thumb and index finger.

Six shivered in the afternoon sun.

Chapter 42

~~

Halekulani Resort, Honolulu, HI
29 Oct, 1500 hours

SIX COULDN'T RELAX. TRY as she might. Her skin burned. Her fingers itched. Anxiety raced along her nerves. Something was very wrong. She could sense it. Feel it like a darkness hovering just beyond the horizon. She glanced over at Ten, who appeared half-asleep in his beach chair.

"We should go find Ben," she said, voicing the fear she'd kept at bay for the twenty minutes since he'd left. Something about Ben's demeanor bothered her, but she couldn't pinpoint it. "Something's wrong. I know it."

Ten cracked one of his eyes open. "Would you take it easy? Miller's a pro. You know that as well as I do. I'm sure he's fine." He tapped the cellphone on the small table next to them. "Besides, if anything happened, he would call me for backup. I'm his partner."

She almost laughed but stopped herself. Instead she glanced at the phone, and then back at Ten. "You have to trust me on this. Ben's in trouble."

The kid sighed. "You're not going to let it go, are you?"

She shook her head.

He blew out a long breath. "Fine. We'll go find Miller. But you're taking the full blame," he warned. "I am only following your orders. You'll tell Miller that before he kicks my ass, right?"

"Deal."

⊕

THE ASSASSIN SMILED AS his prey slipped into reach. Hannah Winslow would die, and soon. He wouldn't fail again. He'd take her slow, make her beg for mercy. The bitch deserved it, after all. She'd nearly destroyed everything. But he'd have his revenge. His mission would be complete.

His boss would be proud.

⊕

THE RENTAL CAR BOUNCED along the dirt road sending Six crashing into the passenger side window as Ten swerved to avoid yet another pothole. "Anybody on this island ever hear of blacktop?" he said, narrowly missing another crater in the road.

"Are you sure we're going the right way?" she asked, scanning the dense, lush greenery surrounding them. For the last mile or so, since they'd turned off the main road, a lump had started to form in her stomach. The sense of wrongness that had assailed her earlier grew into full-on panic as they drove farther and farther from the resort.

Ten didn't seem to share her fears; instead he hummed some inane tune that grated on her last nerve. She repeated her question, spotting the perfect place for an ambush ahead as the road dipped sharply toward a deep ravine.

If she wanted to take out a target, she'd set up on the ridge above. Once she spotted the vehicle, she'd fire a round straight through the driver's side window, forcing the car off the road and into the ravine. Or maybe slice the brake lines to slowly bleed out, making the whole thing look like an accident. The target wouldn't know what hit them. No mercy. No chance of escape. Her fingers tightened on the door handle.

Damn you, Ben. Don't you dare die on me, she thought as yet another wave of fear swept over her. "Curtis, are you sure these are the directions you gave Ben?"

Before he could respond, she yanked the wheel of the car, sending it fishtailing. The tires skidded on the gravel, threatening to send the car over the edge of the cliff. Dust flew up, nearly obscuring the roadway.

"What the fuck?" Ten yelled, as they stopped on the edge of the ravine.

Smoke curled up from the depths of the gully. Six leapt from the vehicle, her sandals sinking into the soft earth. Her hand flew to her mouth. "Call nine-one-one," she yelled, her eyes locked on the twisted wreckage of a vehicle below.

Chapter 43

❧

Wɪᴛʜ ɴᴏ ᴛʜᴏᴜɢʜᴛ ꜰᴏʀ her own safety, Six ran toward the edge of the ravine, searching for the safest and fastest way down to the devastation below.

As she started down the embankment, Ten reached for her arm and jerked her up. She stumbled but caught herself, her eyes never leaving the smoldering Jeep below.

Ben's Jeep.

"We have to help him!" she screamed. "Hurry. Get a rope. Call the paramedics. Do something!"

"Why would I do that?" Ten said with a laugh.

A much too familiar laugh.

Her body went cold as her heart slammed wildly in her chest. She glanced up from the wreckage of the Jeep to the smiling face of an assassin.

Ten pointed a 9mm at her, all boyish naiveté gone. She stared into the dead eyes of a professional killer. To make matters worse, the gun in his hand was her own. The one Ben had slipped her two days ago. A shiny new Glock.

She would've laughed at the irony if Ben hadn't been lying in the wreckage below. Now her only goal was to stay alive long enough to save him. "Why?" she asked, her voice barely above a whisper. "Ben trusted you."

"Not quite," he said with a laugh, the same insane laugh as the assassin from the stairwell. The son-of-a-baby-assassin-bitch had tried to kill her, not once, but twice before.

And had likely killed Ben.

Rage, white and hot in its intensity, sharpened her mind and put all her instincts on alert, awakening the side of her capable of cold, efficient violence. She took a step toward Ten. "You should shoot me now," she said through clenched teeth.

"You don't get off that easy, Hannah. You and I are going to spend some time getting to know each other first." He withdrew a handheld device no bigger than a cellphone from his pocket with his free hand. Her eyes narrowed on the black box. He grinned. "You see this little thingy here?" He waved the device around. "Know what it is?"

Her eyes traveled from the device to the twisted metal of Ben's Jeep. She nodded slowly. "It's a remote control."

"Good girl." He took a step closer, his finger hovering over the black button. "One little press of this here button and your lover or what's left of him," he chuckled, "goes boom."

She closed her eyes. "Who sent you to kill me? OPS?"

He tucked the gun into his waistband and grabbed her arm, yanking her off her feet and into his body. His hot breath on the back of her neck made her stomach crawl. "OPS is a steady paycheck, but this," he ran his hand over her breast, "is a little side project for someone willing to pay a lot more than OPS to see you dead."

"You're a mercenary."

He laughed. "Oh, baby, I don't do mercy." He slammed her headfirst into the hood of the rental car. Blood exploded from her mouth as her teeth cut into the tender flesh of her lips. Pain stole her ability to breathe, to think, as blackness seeped into her vision and her head bounced off hard metal.

But he was far from finished. He ground his body into her

back, crushing her farther and farther into the hood. "Do you like that, Hannah?" he asked.

Rather than answer, she threw her elbow backward, hoping to break a rib or two. He saw it coming, blocking her arm with his. "I know all your little tricks." He laughed. "Both you and Miller thought you were so smart, always ordering me around. Go here. Do this. Well, who's in control now?"

He ground her body further into the metal, denting the vehicle. Ten was the kind of assassin who enjoyed the game, the violence. He would love to hear her scream. But she wouldn't give him the satisfaction. He'd have to hurt her very badly first.

The ringing of a cellphone stopped his assault. The assassin pushed her against the vehicle, holding her in place with his free hand as he checked the caller ID. "Excuse me, Hannah, but I need to take this. You know how it is, when duty calls ...." He pressed the talk button on his phone. "I have her," he said to the caller.

The crackle of static reached Six's ears, but she couldn't make out the speaker's words or identify his voice.

"Yeah," Curtis said into the phone. "I took care of Miller too. Just like you ordered."

Tears welled in Six's eyes. He couldn't be dead. Not Ben. Like her damn cat, he had nine lives. Her eyes flickered to the deep ravine still smoking from the wreckage.

Ten ended his call, quickly forcing Six to her feet. His thick, dirty fingers dug into her flesh, sending waves of revulsion through her. "Let's have a little fun, shall we? After all, you owe me," he said as he twisted her arm behind her back, nearly separating her arm from her shoulder.

Six slammed her head back, connecting with his face. In retaliation he forced her face to the hood once again. Six swallowed a hot rusty rush of blood.

"Never would've guessed that you'd like the rough stuff. I'm willing enough." He chuckled, smashing into the car again as he withdrew a large Army-issued knife from its sheath at his waistband. He pressed the knife to her cheek. "I'm going to make you beg for death."

Blackness swirled through her vision. In an instant Six knew that she would die here.

Ben's face flashed through her mind.

But not yet.

Not until Curtis Daniels bled.

Summoning every black emotion she had—grief, fear, and rage—she reared again, smashing the back of her head into his face. The crack of bone meeting bone echoed inside her head. This time he released her, staggering back a step.

She spun around, advancing, the prey becoming the predator.

"Not so fast." He stopped her with a laugh, lifting the remote control with one hand while trying to stanch the flow of blood from his busted nose with the other.

She froze, every cell in her body wanted to rip Curtis to shreds, but she couldn't, wouldn't risk Ben's life. If he was still alive. "What do you want from me?" she asked through bloody lips.

"That's easy," he said, his eyes raking her body. "I want you to die," Curtis held up the remote control, a crazy grin distorting his wide face, "like your boyfriend."

"No!" she screamed as he pressed the trigger.

Chapter 44

~

NOTHING HAPPENED.

Ten stabbed the remote again. Again, nothing. A slow smile spread over Six's face. Before she could advance on her target, he yanked the 9mm from his waistband and aimed it at her heart.

She stopped. She could almost smell his fear. He was losing control of his carefully orchestrated assassination. Six knew the feeling. Panic would soon set in, and he would give her the chance she needed. He would die, even if it killed her.

It had started to rain, to pour. Water and blood washed down Ten's bleached face, giving him the marbled look of a side of beef.

"Doesn't matter." He tossed the remote to the ground. "Miller's as good as dead down there. Now it's your turn to join him." His finger began to squeeze the trigger.

She threw herself sideways as the deafening roar of a 9mm broke the silence. Expecting horrific pain, she was pleasantly surprised to feel nothing. No white light greeted her. Surprisingly no smell of brimstone either.

From her spot on the rain-soaked earth, she glanced up and

into the face of an angel, an avenging angel who'd just blown a nice, neat round hole in Curtis Daniel's forehead.

"Ben?" she whispered.

"Hey, sweetheart," he said, bending down next to her. He carefully pulled her into his arms, doing his best to wipe away the blood covering her face. "You scared the shit out of me."

She grinned through her busted lips, her teeth stained red with blood. "I could say the same about you." Pushing him away, she slowly staggered to her feet. "I thought you were dead." She punched him in the arm.

He frowned, his brows knitting with concern over her puny punch. "Why don't we save this discussion for another time?" He held out a hand to steady her. "Right now you need a hospital and I need a really, really big drink."

She started to argue, but the throbbing inside her head won out and she slumped to the ground. Ben caught her in his arms before she landed on her already damaged head.

His lips brushed her bloody forehead as he lifted Ten's cellphone from the ground with his free arm. He stared at the number of the last call. A number Ben was very familiar with. No emotion showed on his face as everything clicked into place. The botched bunny assassination. John Pillars, a practical ghost. The evidence against Six. Parker's orders. The assassination attempts and bombings.

⊕

Somewhere over Chicago, IL, Latitude 41.90, Longitude 87.65
29Oct, 2100 hours

THE HEAVY DRONE OF an airplane engine buzzed around Six, waking her from her concussed slumber. She wanted nothing more than to snuggle deeper into the warmth of oblivion surrounding her, but the rhythmic whine returned her to consciousness. "What the hell?" she said as she opened her one good eye. The other one was swollen shut, as battered as the rest of her face.

Ben glanced down at his former partner and winced. "You look like hell. Here," he said passing her a bottle of prescription pills and a plastic cup of water. "Take two of these and go back to sleep. We'll be landing soon."

"Landing?" she whispered. Rage burned in her chest at yet another betrayal. Even after everything that had happened, he was taking her back to Washington. Back to the very man who tried to kill them both only hours ago. Didn't Ben understand the danger? Was his mission worth his life?

Her entire body felt like a piñata on the sixth of May, so for once, she didn't argue. Instead, she popped open the bottle of painkillers and dry swallowed four tablets.

Once she settled back down in the airplane seat and closed her eyes, Ben reached over and kissed her forehead. "I won't let anyone hurt you."

Except for you, she thought as she drifted off to sleep.

Chapter 45

"WHEN DID YOU SUSPECT Ten was the second assassin?" Six asked an hour later, groggy from the medication, but relieved that her pain had eased to a manageable level. She reclined her airplane seat, gazing out into the night sky. The twinkle of millions of lights a few miles ahead warned her that there wasn't much time left. Washington was fast approaching, and with it, a wealth of new and unexpected problems. Almost all of them related to the man seated next to her.

Damn, she missed her cat. Maybe she did like the mangy creatures after all. With the cat the only thing she needed to worry about was fleas. Ben was a whole other story. The cat didn't lie to her at every turn, use her as bait, or keep her in the dark. The cat didn't make her want things she could never have. She wondered what would happen to the cat when she didn't return to San Diego at the scheduled time. Would the H2 receptionist take him home with her? They had probably bonded by now. Sweetie would be better off with someone committed to his welfare enough to call him by name.

Although he didn't ask much of her, Sweetie would be little comfort in the face of certain death. Ben had saved her life.

But by not telling her that Ten was a threat, he had nearly cost her that life.

One thing was clear. She wasn't Ben's partner or his confidant anymore. He was a stranger.

Maybe he always had been.

When he didn't answer her question, she jabbed her elbow into his ribs, harder this time, and repeated her question. "When did you realize Curtis was the assassin in the stairwell?"

Ben opened his eyes, yawned and stretched. "Does it matter now? He's dead. You're safe." When she glared at him, he sighed. "Fine. I was a little slow on the uptake. Are you happy?"

"No." She poked him again. "When?"

"I suspected him after the bomb. The first bomb. Well not the first. The one in the hotel room." He shook his head. "It was a move right out of CIA 101, which left me with two suspects."

She gasped. "You thought I blew up my own hotel room?"

He winced. "Not for long."

"You never trusted me. Not when OPS burned me. Not after we slept together. Not now." That thought hurt much more than it should, but she pushed past the pain, and focused instead on her anger. Rage was easier. Rage didn't tear at her soul.

Again he winced. "Han—"

"Don't," she said, her voice deadly soft.

He ran a hand through his already messy hair. "I never meant for you to get hurt."

Even drugged to her eyeballs, she could tell when he was lying. "Don't lie to me. Not anymore. You were using me as bait, using me to draw Curtis out. You wanted him to try to kill me again. Admit it."

He blew out a breath as if he'd been holding it for a very long time. "You weren't supposed to get hurt. Addison and Benson were supposed to stop Daniels before …."

She laughed, her voice tinged with bitterness. So many lies. "Did you find what you needed or was my near murder all for naught?"

"No."

"So, what happened this afternoon after you left the resort?" She licked her dry, cracked lips.

The laugh was half-hearted and failed to reach his eyes. "The kid cut my break line. Like I would fall for something as amateurish as that."

"How did your Jeep end up in a ravine then?"

"Fine," he sighed. "I might've been slightly distracted and missed the brake line until it was almost too late."

Distracted? Ben? In the three years they'd worked together, she'd never seen him distracted, even after he found his ex-wife in bed with his accountant.

Before she could ask what had distracted him, he continued, "I realized the kid was making a play so I searched the Jeep and found the bomb. I disarmed it and had started backtracking to the resort when the brakes failed. I had enough time to bail before the Jeep went over the embankment."

"You should've shot the bastard twice," she said, a trickle of blood running from the cut on her mouth.

Wrapping his arm around her, he ignored her protests and pulled her close, kissing the top of her head. "What makes you think I didn't?"

Her eyes narrowed. "How'd you realize he planned to take you out too?" She slapped her leg, answering her own question. "Damn it. The tracking device you implanted in my hip. It saved my life."

"Both our lives." He had the nerve to look happy about it. "When you left the resort, I knew something was wrong. Either the kid had slipped by Addison and Benson and was making a move or—"

"Or what?"

"Never mind."

She grabbed his arm, her fingers digging into his muscle as she forced the words past the lump of sorrow in her throat. "You figured I betrayed you. That I lied and was running again."

He closed his eyes. "Yes."

The sting of the single word seared her heart and sealed his fate.

Chapter 46

Ronald Reagan Airport, Washington, DC
29Oct, 2300 hours

BEN CARRIED A SLEEPING Six into the backseat of a waiting limo. The air in D.C. felt heavy with frost, nothing like the sweet warm air of paradise. His heart gave a small squeeze. Life in Washington couldn't be more different from life in the tropical paradise.

Yet the one thing D.C. and paradise had in common was that someone wanted Hannah dead, and Ben would be damned if he let anyone hurt her again. Just thinking of the moments of terror when Ten had her in his clutches was enough to make the cold, calculated assassin begin to shake.

"Where to?" the driver asked.

Ben glanced at the beautiful, damaged, drugged woman sleeping so peacefully next to him and wanted nothing more than to put her on the next plane to anywhere but here. "Georgetown," he said instead.

⊕

MILES AWAY, IN A hermetically sealed office building in the heart of Washington, Parker Langdon read the latest report from Benjamin Miller. A shiver ran up his neck. Agent Miller was not being exactly truthful about Hannah Winslow's current whereabouts.

That could only mean one thing.

It was time for him to deal with both Hannah Winslow and Miller, and he had to do it quickly.

⊕

THREE DAYS LATER, TUCKED away in a safe house on the outskirts of Georgetown, Six faced off with her former partner. "Ten blew up my condo? How could you not tell me?" Six screeched, pacing in front of Ben. Anger reverberated off her in waves. "Anything else you forgot to mention? Maybe a plague or two?"

He reached for her arm, but she yanked it away. "It wasn't intentional. I simply forgot."

She whirled around on him. "You forgot?"

"I was a little busy keeping you alive, if you remember."

Six remembered all right. She remembered how he'd forced her to return to D.C., used her as bait, lied to her at every opportunity, and even implanted a tracking device on her body. As much as she wanted to smack him, a part of her wanted nothing more than for him to take her in his arms.

She punched him in the chest instead.

"Hey," he said, rubbing his chest. "What was that for?"

Rather than answer she hit him again. He quickly stood, grabbing her arms, and pulling her against his warm, muscular chest. For a few seconds, she struggled, hating the way he made her feel. Hating even more the way she felt about him.

Well, it was time for Ben to suffer at her hands for a change. She suddenly stopped struggling, turning soft and pliant in his arms. Her fingers curled around his neck, dragging his mouth to hers. Their kiss was anything but sweet. Six's tongue plundered his mouth, stroking his with the rhythmic pattern as old as time.

The palm of his hands slid up her back, pushing her deeper into his heat. The ridged outline of his erection jutted into her stomach, turning her body molten with desire.

She moaned low and deep in her throat, spurring him on. He cupped her bra-less breasts through the rough fabric of her T-shirt, and her nipples puckered, sharpening into twin points of desire. His knee worked its way between her hot thighs, pushing into her liquid core as his tongue matched the quick friction of hers.

Bodies burning with lust, the two assassins charged to the brink, until Ben broke the kiss, pulling away, his breath coming in short gasps. "I want you," he said.

"Good," she responded, equally out of breath. But she was far from finished. Her fingers curved in the hem of her T-shirt, slowly lifting the material in an erotic striptease. Her tanned, toned stomach appeared, followed by the curve of her breasts.

He averted his gaze, taking a step back, his mouth suddenly as dry as the desert. "We can't do this," he said, as regretful as a man refusing his favorite meal. "There's too much at stake to risk it on casual sex."

Casual sex? Nothing was casual about the way Ben touched her body. He branded her. Forcing her to submit. Forcing her to feel. A sick longing assailed her.

"We need to think about this logically."

Six cocked her head skeptically. Her heart ached so much that she actually placed a hand on her chest, as if touching it might contain the hurt. "That didn't seem to stop you a few days ago."

She dropped her T-shirt back in place. Her heart shattered as the truth dawned on her. Sleeping with her was casual for him—a part of the job. A means to an end, like using her as bait to catch Daniels. And she'd fallen for it. Worse, she'd fallen in love. How stupid could she be?

He held up his hands to ward off her attack, but she stopped short of physical harm. "I—"

Before he could finish his statement or see the tears burning her eyes, she spun on her heels and ran up the stairs, slamming the bedroom door behind her. Ben stared after her, regret and longing clearly etched on his face.

Chapter 47

~

Georgetown Safe House, Washington, D.C.
1 Nov, 1600 hours

SIX SAT ON THE edge of the guestroom bed, her legs crossed at the ankles, as she contemplated her next move. Staying with Ben was no longer an option.

He didn't love her. He never would. He considered their relationship a casual affair. Sex without strings. To him she was nothing more than a mission with benefits.

Nothing more than a number.

And she would never be anything more. No matter how much she tried to be or longed for it.

As blasé as he appeared about her over the last three days, she knew he would not simply let her walk out the door. Her still healing lips hardened into a bitter smile. Nothing had changed over the past few days except the locale.

Why fight the inevitable?

It was time to face the music or at least the maestro.

⊕

Hours later, Ben took a swig of beer from a long-necked bottle and scowled into the darkness. He pictured Hannah's face when he'd called what they had casual sex. The hurt in her eyes when he'd pushed her away this afternoon nearly destroyed his resolve. She'd looked so beautiful, yet sad, yellowing bruises around her eyes. He hated causing her more pain.

But he had vowed to protect her, mostly from himself. He owed her. He'd endangered her enough already. He wouldn't make the same mistake again. Until all of this was over, he would keep his hands to himself, even if it killed him. She deserved that much.

She deserved much better than him.

⊕

OPS Headquarters, Washington, D.C.
2Nov, 0900 hours

STAYING ALIVE WAS SIX's main goal when she stepped through the glass doors and into the opulent marble and chrome hallway of OPS early the next morning. She looked neither right nor left, but walked purposefully toward the elevators at the end of the corridor, her four-inch heels clicking against the polished floor in a steady rat-tat-tat.

A guard at the security desk by the glass doors, about ten-feet away, dressed in full uniform and tactical gear, stopped her as she neared the elevator. "Excuse me, miss," he called.

She took a steady breath, slowly turning to face him. Her heart slammed in her chest, but she managed to plaster a thin smile on her face.

"Oh," the guard said. "I didn't realize it was you, Ms. Young," he said, referring to Parker Langdon's administrative assistant. The woman whose identity Six was currently borrowing.

Wearing a jet black, shoulder length wig, a charcoal gray designer dress suit, and matching gray pumps, Six passed for

Kim Young—at a distance. Add a pair of dark sunglasses and a stolen ID lanyard and the transformation was complete.

The elevator opened, and she stepped inside, letting out a relieved breath to find it empty. She slipped Ben's ID card from her pocket. The same card she'd managed to swipe from his wallet last night.

Getting the card proved easier than she'd thought. He'd seemed oblivious to her theft, reclining in an easy chair, the television on, beer bottles scattered around him. An empty six-pack.

Something had him rattled. That much was clear.

Whatever it was, Six needed to stay focused on the problem at hand and not the painful squeeze her heart gave every time she thought about Ben and his lying lips.

She needed to stay alive long enough to find Davis' killer and the person who'd ruined her life. She had one lead—Parker Langdon.

Six slid Ben's card key ID through the security slot and pressed number eleven. The elevator doors slowly closed behind her. For a second she sagged against the wall, taking a deep breath in the tight-fitting business suit. How the hell did Kim Young get through a day? Six hated wearing nylons almost as much as she'd hated spending three days wearing a smelly beaver costume in 107 degree heat.

Numbers flashed by on the elevator console. She checked the mag of the 9mm tucked into the waistband of her skirt. 7 ... 8 ... 9 ... 10. One more floor to go.

One last moment to nurse a lifetime's worth of regrets.

The elevator dinged as it arrived on the eleventh floor. The doors opened with a whoosh of stale office air. She quickly glanced around, scanning the interior of the cubicle maze for anyone who might intend to do her harm. Luckily for her, only a skeleton administrative staff sat at their desks, their attention riveted on flickering computer screens.

Six picked her way through the maze of cubicles, her goal

the big office on the far side of the building. A few of the secretaries gave her a vague, half-hearted wave as she passed, fully concentrating on the data their screens displayed.

At the end of the long corridor stood a larger desk, this one reserved for the woman Six was pretending to be. The same woman who would be delayed this morning after she awoke to four flat tires on her shiny Prius.

One obstacle now stood between Six and her goal, the tired face of Paul Fuller. Parker's second-in-command stood poised at the director's door, a coffee cup in his hand and a grim expression on his face.

Was the jig up? Had someone recognized her and alerted Fuller? *Stop being paranoid*, she ordered herself. If OPS had even an inkling of her whereabouts they'd shoot first and worry about collateral damage later. Yet, even in her heightened state, Six recognized the look in Paul's eyes—frustration bordering on desperation.

Taking a deep breath, she walked toward Fuller, expecting the worst, but he didn't seem to notice her. Instead, he glanced at Parker's closed office door, shook his head, and walked away. She smiled. Sometimes it paid to be invisible, especially for an assassin in uncomfortable four-inch heels.

Pulling the 9mm from her waistband, she reached for the brass doorknob of Parker's office. This was it. Do or die. Literally. In the next few moments she would either learn the truth about Davis' death or find herself butt-deep in bullets.

The latter option held little appeal. But she'd be damned if she spent another night of her life hiding. Parker Langdon would either spill the beans or his blood.

Chapter 48

~

"IT'S YOUR MOVE," PARKER Langdon said, his phone pressed tightly to his ear. "You either do what's right, or I send a team to do it for you." Parker frowned as the person on the other end of the line spoke. "That's right," he said when the speaker paused. "This is your last chance. Now do what you were paid to do." Parker punctuated his statement by slamming down the phone. "Idiot," he muttered to himself.

His office door opened, drawing his attention to the woman standing there. "Kim," he began, "I told you not to interrupt …." He trailed off when he realized it wasn't Kim in the doorway, but an armed assassin, her 9mm pointed at his head.

"Hello, Parker," Six said, her voice light. "Been awhile."

"Hannah," Parker responded, his eyes on the weapon in her hand. "We've been looking for you. Glad to see you're still in one piece."

"No thanks to you," Six said, flatly, as if they were discussing the unseasonably warm weather rather than contracted murder.

Parker leaned forward, his hands slowly moving toward

his desk drawer, where a panic button was hidden. "Now Hannah—"

"Don't," she said, her finger tightening on the trigger. Parker leaned back, his hands moving to the highly polished desk top. Six stepped farther into the room, removing her wig and dark glasses. "I want to see the evidence against me," she said. "Now."

Parker snorted a small, bitter laugh. "Shoot me and you'll never get out of here alive." He pushed himself slowly away from the desk and rose to his feet, towering over Six, even in her four-inch heels. "We both know it. So why don't you turn yourself in?"

It was Six's turn to laugh. "That would make things so easy for you, wouldn't it?" With the barrel of her gun, she motioned for Parker to sit. He did, reluctantly, crossing his arms in front of him. She continued, "Rogue agent tied neatly up with a bow. And the cherry on top? No more messy investigation into you and your company. Really a win-win."

Parker nodded slowly. "It's the right thing to do."

She dropped down in the chair directly across from him, the gun never wavering from its target. Dead center of Parker's chest. "But there is one small problem."

"Oh?" Parker said, the sneer in his tone as transparent as the double pane glass windows that sealed the two adversaries inside. "And what's that?"

Six tilted her head as if weighing how much to tell him. Parker's face was flushed with anger. There sat a woman who'd been accused of murdering a fellow agent in cold-blood and nearly destroying the company Parker held so dear. A woman his best agents had tracked halfway around the world. A woman who had cost him more than she would ever know.

"I didn't kill Davis."

Parker snorted.

"But, Parker," she leaned forward, her eyes boring into his, "I can prove it."

He closed his eyes for a brief second, and then shook his head. A thin smile formed on his lips as his fingers curled around the small-caliber Ruger LCP 380 pistol holstered under his desk. "Hannah," he said with genuine regret. "I really wish you hadn't said that."

Chapter 49

~~~

Georgetown Safe House, Washington, D.C.
2Nov, 1000 hours

Benjamin Miller woke to a buzzing in his brain. No matter how he tried to block it, the pain continued down his spine and along his every nerve ending, much like an electrical current through faulty wiring. Just when the vibrations appeared to stop, they started again, growing stronger and stronger.

He groaned, forcing one eye open against the pounding pain. An empty beer bottle lay shattered on the floor next to him. The stench of stale beer wafted from the crushed mess, turning his already sour stomach. Choking back a wave of nausea, he slowly opened his other eye. When God failed to be merciful and kill him outright, he flopped onto his back like a fish out of water.

Blinking up at the ceiling, he strove valiantly to piece together the events of the last few hours. To the casual observer, his situation was all too clear. A late-night bender and the subsequent hangover. Take two aspirins and call it a day. But Ben could only wish he was drunk. So drunk that the embarrassment and rage buried just under the pain would be a fading memory.

Unfortunately for him, forgetting was not an option, and neither was spending another minute on the beer-soaked carpet waiting for his body to recover from the shock of a lifetime.

Not with Six on the loose.

His hand clenched into a slack fist; his fingers failed to respond to his brain's command to flex. *Damn her*. Why couldn't she trust him? Just this once. He winced, knowing the answer even as he posed the question.

Why trust him when he'd failed to believe in her?

He'd needed a couple of days at the most, and then all of this would be over. But Six hadn't waited. Instead she'd tased him with fifty thousand volts and vanished into the city.

This wasn't quite what he had expected from his morning. In fact, he'd woken up feeling pretty damn good, even after indulging in a few beers the night before as he tried to forget the taste of her. The memories of her soft skin. Of the low, purring moans she made when he touched her.

Whistling tunelessly, he'd gone about his morning routine, throwing on a pair of basketball shorts and beginning a grueling workout. A thousand sit-ups later, sweat poured from his body as his mind focused on breathing through five hundred one-armed pushups.

Three hundred and twenty-four pushups in, Six strolled down the stairs, her hair pulled tightly into a bun, dark eyeliner circling her eyes, giving her an almost Asian appearance. Ben paused in his routine, enjoying the way her legs looked in her pencil skirt. "Morning," he said, his breath even and deep. Not for long though.

She'd crossed the room, stopping in front of him, her legs at eyelevel. Ben's heartbeat sped up as his pumping blood slipped south. Her fingers reached for his arm, slowly pulling him to his feet. He came more than willingly. He started to speak, but she pressed her fingers to his lips.

He nodded, understanding her need for silence. So much was between them. So many questions unanswered. So many lies and half-truths. So much mistrust and pain.

Brushing her fingers over his face she'd wrapped her arms around the back of his neck, pulling him to her lips. His mouth touched hers, slowly at first, but gaining pressure and need.

His resolve not to touch her crumbled instantly. He swept her into his arms, pressing his sweaty body against hers with days of pent-up desire. His breathing hitched as Six returned his embrace with equal parts lust and something more. Something that had them both on edge. At the time Ben had believed it was passion, but now he knew the truth. She was saying goodbye.

For good.

Electricity crackled between them, pushing him to the abyss between want and need. For once in his life he allowed the walls around his heart to weaken and somehow Six had managed to wiggle inside. Lust was one thing, but this was something more. Something that went beyond the chemical. Beyond electric. Six pulled away for a brief moment. Their eyes locked.

And then she tased him with fifty-thousand volts.

The buzzing returned, dragging him to the present. This time he recognized the sound. His cellphone. Feeling around on the ground, he located the phone underneath him, which explained the buzzing. At least he hoped that explained it.

"Yeah," he answered, his voice sounding as rough as rock-gut whiskey.

"Miller? Is that you?" Paul Fuller asked through the cell static. His voice sounded odd to Ben's ears. A feeling of dread crawled up Ben's spine. "You need to get down to OPS. Now," Paul said.

Ben closed his eyes. "What happened?"

"There's been a shooting."

Chapter 50

~

OPS Headquarters, Washington, D.C.
2Nov, 1100 hours

Bᴇɴ ᴘᴜsʜᴇᴅ ᴛʜʀᴏᴜɢʜ ᴛʜᴇ crowded office building, his
eyes scanning the myriad of faces along the corridor,
some frozen with shock, others dazed from fear. Violence had
that effect. Even on people who lived with it daily.

With each step his heart grew heavier. Whatever lay beyond
Parker Langdon's closed office door, he vowed not to let his
emotions show. Please, he prayed, but he knew the truth. After
this morning everything had changed.

Parker's assistant, Kim, stood in front of the doorway, her
face pale but otherwise stony. His gut clenched tighter. She
held up her hand. "You can't go in there."

Ignoring her, he shoved the door wide. The unmistakable
scent of death and the rusty odor of blood assailed his senses.
Taking a shallow breath through his mouth he stepped farther
into the room, closer to the body hidden under the sheet on
the floor.

Paul stood next to the body, his face grim. "I'm glad you came."

"What happened?" Ben asked, moving around the room, careful not to disturb the body or compromise the already compromised crime scene. This wasn't typical workplace violence. The cops wouldn't be called. Detectives wouldn't arrive in rumpled dark suits. Witnesses would be silenced. A murder would be swept under the rug. By all appearances a killer would go free.

"Clear the room," Paul said to the team of agents collecting evidence inside Parker's office. They stopped working and filed out. None of them met Ben's gaze. Paul waited until the door closed behind the last agent before he spoke. "Surveillance video shows that at 0900 an armed-intruder slipped past security."

"Six."

"Yes," he said. "Hannah used your security credentials to take the elevator to the eleventh floor. Soon after, shots were fired."

"And?" Ben's voice never wavered even as his heart squeezed in his chest. The fear that Hannah lay beneath the sheet stole his ability to breathe. To think. To function. *I can't lose her now*, he thought.

Eyes on Ben's face, Paul lifted the sheet from the body, exposing the very pale and very dead face of the OPS director, Parker Langdon. Two small entry wounds, dead center of his chest, were the only sign of violence.

Relief filled Ben, followed instantly by guilt. Parker was his boss, had a family, friends. His death was not to be taken lightly. Yet it wasn't Hannah under the sheet. He could barely control the joy rushing through him. Leaning down, his face without expression, he examined the entry wounds.

For a few minutes the only sound in the room was the drone of the furnace. Then Ben broke the silence with one word. "Assassination."

"What?"

Slowly Ben gained his feet, his muscles still sore from their earlier abuse. "This was planned. Not a crime of passion or anger. This was an assassination."

Now Paul bent down, his forehead wrinkling. "My God," he said. "You're right. I didn't see these before." He gestured to the faint line around Parker's wrists. The killer had restrained Parker shortly before his death. The look in Paul's eyes said it all. He blamed Hannah for Parker's murder.

Try as he might, Ben couldn't come up with another plausible suspect at the moment. "Where is she?" he asked, his voice much calmer than the raging emotions inside him. He needed to see Six, to hear her side of things, to find the truth behind what looked like cold-blooded murder. He'd unfairly condemned her once and it had nearly killed her. He'd be damned before he made that mistake again.

Paul swallowed, staring out the window at the busy street below. "We don't know."

"How is that possible?" He stepped forward. "Someone heard the shots, right? Someone had to see her." His heartbeat accelerated. What if one of those shots had struck Six? What if, right now, she was hurt or worse? The thought sent a chill down his spine.

Paul turned back to face Ben, his eyes frosty. "Enough is enough. It ends today. I want Hannah Winslow brought in." He paused, his eyes drifting toward Parker's bloodless face. "Dead or alive."

Chapter 51

◆~◆

Hi-Low Motel, Washington, D.C.
2 Nov, 1700 hours

ON THE OTHER SIDE of the city, in a run-down motel where customers paid by the hour, Six sat on a stained bedspread, her 9mm tucked between the pillow and headboard. A cockroach scurried across the floor, its antennae twitching as if receiving radio signals from alien life forms.

I'm losing my mind, she thought, closing her eyes. Her eyelids felt like sandpaper left in the desert too long. Taking a long drink from her Starbucks extra-large, six shot espresso, she again focused on the file folder in her hands.

Report after report told of sordid dealings and bribes. The evidence against her weighed a good five pounds and would take her the better part of a week to get through.

So far the file read much like a 1940s noir, featuring her as the lead femme fatale. The first report, a financial spreadsheet baffling to anyone without a C.P.A., listed bank transfers in large amounts of money from John Pillars' Cayman Island account to Six's meager savings. An account that was no longer so meager. In fact, if OPS hadn't frozen all of her assets, she would've been one hell of a rich woman.

Try as she might, she was unable to find any clues in the pages and pages of financials. Whoever had framed her had done a thorough job. By the time she finished the first set of reports she wondered if she was indeed guilty.

Everything looked so convincing, on the surface.

One question kept plaguing her: *Why me?* What made her the perfect scapegoat? Was it her relationship with Davis? Or something more? And why manufacture this elaborate setup? What did John Pillars have to gain by framing her so completely?

Shaking her head, she fought off the urge to curl up and take a much needed nap. But she couldn't stop now. Not when everything depended on uncovering the truth. Soon Ben or an OPS agent much like him would knock on her door, and her time would be up. Her freedom, certainly, and probably her life.

With a sigh she flipped to the next report.

⊕

BEN STOOD IN THE middle of the guest room where Six had slept the night before. It smelled of her. Of lavender and desire. Of determination and spice. His heart gave a small squeeze as he cursed himself once again for letting her go. His fear for her grew with each passing minute. Parker was dead and she appeared to be the only suspect, at least according to OPS.

He'd spent the better part of the afternoon watching surveillance of the hour before Parker's death until three hours after. The video showed Six arriving at OPS dressed as Kim Young. Entering the elevator in full disguise, using his ID card. Going into Parker's office.

And then nothing.

According to the video feed, no one entered or left Parker's office for the next four hours. Not until the real Kim arrived late for work and found Parker's body.

Hour after hour of video proved nothing.

Would she kill Parker in cold blood? Maybe if she saw him as a threat. Ben frowned, picturing the phone number on Ten's cellphone. Was Six right? Was OPS out to kill her? Or was John Pillars pulling the strings? Was Parker's death all part of some grand scheme, a scheme involving the woman Ben couldn't seem to forget? Was she a victim or a cold-blooded killer?

His gaze fell on the dresser and the small silver tracking device once embedded in Six's skin. It flashed like a beacon in the afternoon sunlight. Next to the device lay a quickly scribbled note in her flowery handwriting:

"Numbers don't lie."

Chapter 52

~~

Eight hours later, long after the sun had gone down, Six still sat on the sagging motel room bed, reading report after report under a dim 40 watt light bulb. She was jittery from too much caffeine, anxiety, and the prospect of having to disprove a pack of lies deep enough to bury her. Throwing the file on the bed, she jumped to her feet. Someone had gone to a lot of trouble to destroy her career and her life.

She ran a hand through her hair, willing the exhaustion, hopelessness, and despair away. She should be searching for clues and analyzing every shred of information in the files, but her mind refused to focus; instead, she thought of Ben. Of the look of betrayal in his face as fifty thousand volts rocked his body.

Pain flooded through her. She missed Ben's smile and the wicked sparkle in his eyes. "Damn you," she said, shoving the file off the bed. As paper flew in all directions, she felt a perverse satisfaction, as if destroying the order of the case against her would somehow free her from its clutches.

But her relief was short-lived. Making a mess of the files wouldn't help her find the clues she needed. Embarrassed by her outburst, she quickly gathered up the scattered reports. Her fingers wrapped around one particular set of papers. An autopsy report from Davis' murder.

A report she'd avoided for the past hour.

Her stomach roiled and she began to shake. Emotions and sensations from that day, so clear in her memory, threatened for the moment to overwhelm her. Smelly fake beaver fur. The gun so right in her hands as she pulled the trigger. Blood and brain matter. The speeding Jeep. The bomb. The look in Ben's eyes when she glanced into the rearview mirror. Ben. It always came back to him. Would she ever forget the feel of his hands on her body? Or the way he'd saved her life even when he believed the worst?

Taking a deep breath, she scanned the report in her hand. A report detailing what little was left of Davis Karter following the explosion. Tears welled in her eyes. The blast and subsequent fire obliterated Davis' remains, so much so that his family had only a handful of ashes to bury. Evidence technicians listed every identifiable bit of Davis, of the Jeep, of the three bullet fragments recovered at the scene.

She reread the last entry.

"It can't be," she said, her hands shaking as she read the report again, this time out loud. "Recovered at the scene: fragment of a .50 caliber weapon as well as two fragments from a smaller, as of yet undetermined caliber weapon."

She dropped on the bed, her knees no longer able to support her weight. "Do you know what this means?" she asked the empty room.

For the first time in six months she felt a glimmer of hope as the weight of Davis' death eased from her heart. She rose from the bed, pulled open the heavy curtains, and smiled into the dark night before returting to the file with a renewed sense of hope.

✛

Perk Coffee Shop, Washington, D.C.
3Nov, 0800 hours

"Have you found Hannah yet?" Paul asked Ben the next
morning as the two sat in a coffee shop in Georgetown.
Morning commuters chugged cups of coffee as they hurried
to their office cubicles with depressing green lighting and stale
donuts left over from the day before.

Ben watched a group of women in expensive dresses and
running shoes file by the window. One woman shot him an
interested smile. He gave her a vague half-smile in return, his
mind firmly occupied by Hannah.

Last night seemed endless to the once unflappable assassin.
Try as he might, he couldn't get Hannah out of his head. Where
the hell was she? Was she hurt? Scared? Lonely?

Had she given up on him?

As he lay awake, something else started to bother him.
Something about Parker's murder. Something he just couldn't
put a finger on.

Paul snapped his fingers to gain Ben's attention, and then
repeated his question. "Any luck tracking Hannah down? We
need to find her, and fast, Ben." He pounded his fist on the table,
toppling his nearly empty cup. A small puddle of black liquid
spilled out, which Paul quickly wiped away with a napkin.
"I'm sorry," he said, righting the cup. "This whole situation
is making me crazy. Parker was more than just my boss. He
was my friend." He paused, his voice thick with emotion. "A
mentor. Hell, the guy trained me on how to be an agent."

"Parker was a good man," Ben lied. The guy would've sold
his own mother into prostitution to get what he wanted. A part
of Ben approved of that sort of greed. It sure as hell beat getting
shot at for your mother country and paid very little for the
privilege.

Maybe Six had the right idea all along. Find some tropical
paradise and forget about making the world a better place. Find

a nice climate, settle down, and make love under the warm afternoon sun. Forget the greater good. Forget taking orders from assholes like Parker. Forget the pain of being betrayed by those you trusted.

Forget Hannah Winslow.

If only he could.

Chapter 53

〜

BEN EXCUSED HIMSELF, LEAVING Paul sitting at a small table sipping burnt coffee. With both regret and affection, the new leader of OPS watched his best assassin disappear toward the back of the shop. Whatever happened with Hannah had taken a toll on the once-jaded assassin. Ben wasn't the same man. And Paul was worried. He needed Ben sharp and alert, for finding Hannah Winslow was priority number one.

The longer Hannah stayed on the run the more anxious Paul grew. But more importantly, what would happen when Hannah ran out of places to hide? Could he trust Ben to deal with her in the end? For bringing Hannah in was no longer an option.

Ben had new orders.

Shoot on sight.

⊕

Hi-Low Motel, Washington, D.C.
3Nov, 0800 hours

SIX STARED AT THE pay-as-you-go burner phone in her hand and counted to ten. *Just dial the damn number*, she ordered her fingers, which refused to comply. What if Ben refused her call like he had the last time?

She needed him now like never before.

Would he help or betray her?

"Please, Ben, for once, just trust me." Swallowing hard, she dialed.

⊕

The phone on the table top vibrated against the Formica, jiggling the empty coffee cup next to it. He glanced down at the number. Rather than answer he sent the caller directly to voicemail.

⊕

"Leave a message at the beep," the automated voice requested with robotic politeness. Six's eyes filled with tears. She quickly swiped them away. When the beep sounded, she spoke. Just two words. "I know."

⊕

Ben sat inside a beige Prius hatchback, his knees practically to his chest, the engine idling on the ice-slick street. What the car lacked in room it more than made up for in giving him the ability to blend in with thousands of other politically correct lobbyists who drove around Georgetown with briefcases full of political bribes. Yet Ben's sights weren't set on nefarious political deeds but rather an assassin.

The words 'shoot to kill' reverberated in his head. His mission was clear. Take the shot. Kill the target. End the game. Dread filled his heart but at this point he had no choice. More innocent people would die unless he completed his mission. People like Parker Langdon. It was time for him to put away his girlie fantasies of a happily-ever-after and finish his mission.

Hannah's kiss-swollen lips and lust-heavy eyelids swam before his mind's eye, aggravating the pain of what was to come. He closed his eyes, trying desperately to hold onto her face, if only for a moment. The roar of a car engine up the block ruined the moment. His eyes flew open and he slid the Prius into gear. Time to complete his mission.

Shoot on sight.

Shoot to kill.

Chapter 54

~~

SIX HUNG UP THE phone, and then, almost as an afterthought, threw it across the room, smiling a little when it made a satisfying dent in the ancient drywall. Ben had refused her call. Again. What was wrong with her? Keeping her faith in him had become an exercise in futility. He'd never made her a single promise. No vow of love. Of trust. Whatever was between them was merely in her head. He'd more than made that clear the night before with his casual sex statement.

Yet that fact didn't change anything. She needed him, or at least his help, because—whether Benjamin Miller participated—she was about to unveil a killer.

Taking a steadying breath, she once again flipped through the thick file of evidence, pausing on one page in particular, a photograph shot through a long lens. A picture of a man. A known associate of the ghost-like John Pillars. The image was grainy and blurred, but Six recognized his face all the same.

⊕

Parking lot of Hi-Low Motel, Washington, D.C.
3Nov, 2200 hours

IN THE DARKNESS, A man inside a small beige car watched
Room 102, his fingers stroking the cold metal of his .9mm,
softly, like a lover. Waiting was part of the game. A game he
would ultimately win. She would die. His mission was clear.
Shoot to kill.

The lights inside the motel room clicked off and the assassin
crept forward. He quickly checked his magazine, readying the
weapon for government-sanctioned murder.

For the greater good.

For his own good.

⊕

SIX YAWNED, SHUTTING OFF the dim motel room light. File in
hand, she moved into the shadows, readying herself for the
night ahead. Exhaustion pulled at her eyelids, weighing them
down. She fought the feeling, but in the end succumbed to
sleep.

⊕

THE HOTEL ROOM DOOR shattered into pieces as the assassin
kicked it in. Bits of wood and metal flew inward like shrapnel,
stabbing into everything in its wake, including the woman
tucked in the corner. Two silenced shots followed, each aimed
directly into the chest of the body under the thin sheet. Dust
and feathers filled the room, choking the air.

Mission complete.

Hannah Winslow was no longer a threat.

The assassin smiled, walking farther into the room. He
pulled a cellphone from his pocket, smiling as the words 'new
voicemail' flickered on the screen.

Hannah Winslow's last words.

He wiped his prints from the phone and then dropped it on the floor next to the bed. As it hit the shag carpet the faint sound of metal against metal reached his ears. He spun toward the new sound, the blood leaving his handsome face.

"I've been waiting for you," Six said from the doorway of the bathroom, her gun leveled at the assassin's head.

Chapter 55

PAUL FULLER PALED SLIGHTLY but otherwise revealed no emotion. But his eyes spoke volumes; he believed he could still accomplish his mission. Hannah Winslow would still die. Six shot him a grim smile, equally eloquent. He could try, but he would die too. Paul lowered his weapon, the barrel facing the grimy carpet.

"Let's talk this out, Hannah. No one needs to die," he said, his tone arrogant. But a slight tremor told Six what she needed to know. Paul Fuller was afraid. Afraid of her, perhaps, but much more likely of what would happen if she lived.

It was all so simple. The last night she'd spent with Davis was the key. That and the photograph of John Pillars' friend. While she and Davis had strolled through the busy Georgetown restaurant district on their date, two men sat inside a quaint, out of the way bistro. Davis must've recognized the gun dealer in the photo as well as the man next to him—John Pillars, aka Paul Fuller—and put two and two together.

After all, at Parker Langdon's request, Davis had spent the last few months studying each member of OPS, looking for the weak link. He'd found his target that night but never had the chance to gather enough evidence to prove that the target Pillar and Fuller were the same man.

Three days later Davis was dead.

Once Six saw the photo, she recalled seeing Fuller and the gun dealer together that night. From there she quickly pieced things together. Fuller arranged for Davis to wear the bunny suit, arranged for her to take the shot, and then planted a bomb to tie everything together in a neat bow, all evidence and assassins buried forever.

"Why?" Six asked, trying to control the hitch in her voice at the innocent murder of a man whose only crime was walking down the wrong street at the wrong time. "You could've explained it away. Davis had no proof."

Paul gave a small laugh. "Davis died because of you." He paused, his eyes on her face as if weighing her reaction. "You pulled the trigger. You killed your lover. No one else."

"You won't get away with this," she said. "Parker knows. He's the one who gave me the file. It's over, Paul."

"That's not quite true." Ben stepped from the shadows of the shattered doorway, his gun on the furious assassin with revenge on her mind.

Keeping her gun trained on Fuller, she barely glanced at Ben, even though her heart leapt at the sound of his voice. 'Too late!' she wanted to scream. She'd needed him hours ago, before the final play started. Now he would only get in the way, maybe even die as Davis had. "Not a good time," she said.

"Yeah, well," he shrugged, "my timing's always sucked. You know that better than anyone."

Paul straightened to his full height. "Agent Miller—"

"Quiet," she snapped, turning her attention to Ben. "You know?" she asked. "About Davis?"

"I know. Karter was already dead by the time you took the shot. Paul killed him and then placed him in our sights." He slowly shook his head. "It was all a setup. The assassination. The Jeep explosion. Everything."

"Including us?"

Ben avoided her question and her gaze.

Paul began, "All well and good—"

Ben swung his gun toward him, silencing him instantly. "Paul arranged for Curtis to become my new partner, and then he sent me off to find you. Daniels' orders were to silence you. When he failed, Paul panicked, especially when he realized Parker was on to him."

Six smiled for the first time since Ben had entered the room. Eyes on Fuller, she said, "Parker will bury you."

Ben winced, and it was Paul's turn to smile. "That's where you're wrong, Hannah." Paul nodded to Ben. "Would you like to tell her or shall I?"

Her face paled. "Parker's dead?"

"Yes, my dear," Paul said. "Yet another notch on your belt."

"No," Ben said, "she didn't kill him." His statement hung in the air. He closed his eyes for a brief second. Lines of pain drew tightly around his mouth. A mouth she'd kissed in what seemed a lifetime ago. Ben faced Fuller. "You killed Parker and then arranged for it to look like Six was to blame. Just like Karter."

"And then he planned to frame you for my murder," she said, pointing to Ben's cellphone on the carpet.

Ben smiled, coldly. "Not a bad idea."

"What I did, I did for the greater good. The gun sales. Parker's death. All of it."

Six snorted.

"You understand, Ben." Paul smiled when Ben nodded. "Parker was moving OPS in the wrong direction. Hannah gave me an opportunity, and I took it." Paul's voice rose with each word as if volume equaled sincerity. "You're a soldier. You know the code. The needs of many outweigh those of the few."

Ben looked away, unable to meet Six's gaze. The sadness on his face nearly undid her. She knew that look. She'd seen it in the mirror many times over the last six months. She took an involuntary step toward Ben, wanting to touch him, to comfort him, to take the pain of what was to come away.

Paul laughed, slowly raising his weapon and aiming directly at her heart. She stopped. His smile widened as he motioned to Ben with his gun. "I believe you have a mission to complete."

Ben gave a barely perceptible nod.

Satisfaction radiated from the new director of OPS. Everything would work out. Hannah Winslow would die. He would be safe once again. He nodded to his favorite assassin. "Make it look like an accident. A drug deal gone bad or something. Nothing leads back to OPS. You know the drill."

"Yes, sir," Ben said.

Six's eyes met Ben's and what she saw there fractured her already battered heart. "No!" she screamed, but it was too late.

Three shots pierced the night air.

Chapter 56

~

Three Blocks from the Hi-Low Motel, Washington, D.C.
4Nov, 0000 hours

AN AMBULANCE SILENTLY PULLED from the motel parking lot, lights dim. There would be no survivors this night. Police tape sealed the scene of what looked very much like a robbery gone bad.

A few blocks away a killer watched from the shadows. He smiled as a body was loaded into the coroner's van. A black body bag surrounded the victim as if protection from further harm. But Paul Fuller was beyond caring. He was dead, killed by two shots to the heart and one to the head.

For good measure.

Fuller never stood a chance. He'd sealed his fate six months before. Ben had finally completed his mission. He'd killed John Pillars. Yet, he felt nothing as he'd pulled the trigger, killing his boss, mentor, and former friend. No guilt. No remorse. Maybe one day regrets would come.

But he doubted it.

Staring into the living and luminous eyes of Hannah

Winslow, he knew he'd made the right decision. For once in his life, he'd made his own choice, the right choice. Orders be damned.

"Why?" Six asked, also watching as Paul Fuller was loaded onto a gurney and carried away. Her eyes reflected something much different. Sadness. Deep, soul-stirring desolation. The look nearly stole his breath away.

He forced his gaze from Six to the crime scene and back again, his chest burning with words his tongue refused to say. He swallowed, focusing on her seemingly innocent question, the subtext riddled with conversational land mines. Hell, he'd rather face a firing squad than this discussion. "He was going to kill you."

"Yeah, he was."

His chest tightened more. "I couldn't let that happen." He reached for her arm, pulling her roughly against him. His eyes burned with desperation. "I'm sorry. For everything. I should've trusted you." He paused. "I do trust you."

"Glad to hear it," she said, her voice trembling with emotion. "So we're more than just casual sex?"

He smiled, but his humor quickly vanished and his eyes grew intent. "You deserve better than a killer like me. You deserve a man who can give you a life filled with love, not death."

"And that's not you?"

He shook his head. "Hell no. I've tried to be logical about my feelings, but damn it, right or wrong, you belong with me. I love you, Hannah Winslow. I've loved you for three years now, and if you let me, I will love you for the rest of our lives."

Hannah pushed away from him to stare into his eyes. "I'm sorry." She brushed her fingers against his lips. "It's just not right."

His heart squeezed in his chest. He'd lost her. "Hannah …." Hands fisted at his sides, the once heartless assassin struggled in vain to control the emotions swirling inside him.

She stared at Ben, thinking of all the things they could have been together, had things only been different. If they hadn't been killers, if he had believed in her. This was what she wanted, wasn't it? To hear him call her by name? To say he loved her, that he had always loved her? She sighed. "Call me Six," she whispered, sealing her words, and their fates, with a kiss.

Epilogue

~~

SOMEWHERE ON A SMALL island in the Pacific Ocean, on April 30th, two lovers lay wrapped in each other's arms as the morning sun rose into the indigo sky. It was just another day in paradise. Waves crashed on the beach a few hundred feet from their bungalow, but the lovers were oblivious to the sound. Their only thoughts were of each other.

And not the danger lurking around the corner. He watched with satisfaction as the dark-haired man kissed the female, and then lay on his back. A perfect target. Unaware. Unprotected.

Slowly he inched forward, stalking his prey.

Ready to take the target down.

And then, in a flash, a blur flew into the lovers' room, attacking with vicious force, rewarded when, and only when, the dark-haired man screamed.

"Damn it, Hannah," Ben said, shoving the twenty pound tabby cat off his chest.

Hannah laughed, watching the struggle between man and beast with amusement. Poor Ben had yet to win one of these wrestling matches with Sweetie. "Come here, baby," she said.

Sweetie did as asked, cutting short his attack on Ben and

settling down in between the lovers, a soft purr bubbling from his throat as Hannah stoked his sleek fur.

Ben frowned down at the cat. "Your cat needs to go on a diet."

Hannah shook her head. "Sweetie isn't my cat, Ben."

"Is that right?"

"He's *our* cat." Hannah leaned over the overgrown cat to kiss her husband of three months, a man who knew her better than she knew herself and yet still loved her. A man willing to kill and die for her, not to mention put up with her cat.

With a sigh, Ben reluctantly agreed, running his hand down Sweetie's back. "In that case, would you ask *our* cat to stop leaving dead mice in my shoes?"

Cindy Miller

J.A. KAZIMER LIVES IN Denver, Colorado. Her other books include *The Junkie Tales*, *The Body Dwellers*, *CURSES! A F***ed-Up Fairy Tale*, *Holy Socks & Dirtier Demons*, *Dope Sick: A Love Story*, *SHANK*, and *Froggy Style*.

When Kazimer isn't looking for the perfect place to hide the bodies, she spends her time surrounded by cats with attitude and a little puppy named Killer. Other hobbies include murdering houseplants, kayaking, snowboarding, reading and theater. After years of slacking, she received a master's degree in forensic psychology, mostly to fill an eight by ten blank space on her wall.

In addition to studying the criminal mind, Kazimer spent a few years spilling drinks on people as a bartender and then wasted another few years stalking people while working as a private investigator in the Denver area.

You can find her online at www.jakazimer.com.

CPSIA information can be obtained at www.ICGtesting.com
Printed in the USA
LVOW12s1716260314

379049LV00001B/87/P